Danny's Corner

Danny's Corner

by

Neil K. Warner

ISBN: 1-55517-494-9
v.1

Published by Bonneville Books

Distributed by:
925 North Main, Springville, UT 84663 • 801/489-4084

Typeset by Virginia Reeder
Cover design by Adam Ford
Cover design © 2000 by Lyle Mortimer

Printed in the United States of America

Dedication

To Jeannie: The loss of one can only be overcome by the love of another

Special thanks to Mom. Why do the words "Thank you," seem like trying to pay for a new car with allowance money? Thanks to Dad—the ultimate copy editor—I miss you. Thanks to Special K, Charmer and Tyke, who wanted me to hurry and finish the airplane story—you're all my Danny's.

Thanks to Kirby, you've helped more than you know and Levor for making the last five years the most enjoyable of my career.

And thanks to Alf Pratte and Jack Nelson the two best professors at BYU next to my dad—sorry.

Finally, to Linda Fincher. I couldn't think of a better title for this book.

Introduction

The last time my wife Jeannie saw her mother alive was on Christmas day. The family received permission to bring her home from the hospital for a day visit after she had been in the hospital for several months. She could not talk. Two strokes had left her speechless. When her mother left her home that day to return to the hospital, she held her children and cried, knowing it would likely be the last time she would see them. Even though she didn't say a word her tears said it all.

Her mother had rheumatic fever when she was a child and it damaged her heart. But she was a fighter and lived through numerous heart attacks and strokes. In January just a few days after my wife's ninth birthday, she passed away.

We often talk about her, but my wife has very few memories of her mother. That's why the last Christmas she spent with her mother is a memory that plays-back in her mind with the frequency of "It's a Wonderful Life" during the holiday season. These memories have helped my wife strive to make the Christmas season one to treasure each year, as she focuses on bringing joy to her own family and also as a remembrance of her mother.

I am always searching for ways to make my wife happy, especially at Christmas because I know what it means to her. As a writer I've written articles for newspapers and magazines for the last ten years, but I've never written anything for her. So I set out to write a Christmas book. After all her favorite things are Christmas and reading so I knew it would be the perfect gift.

I finished just in the "St. Nick" of time. I completed

writing the last page on Christmas Eve. And after running to Wal-Mart to get an ink cartridge just as they were closing the doors, I printed out the last four pages and gave it to her.

One tradition in our family is to open one present on Christmas Eve. I told her she had to open this. By the end of Christmas day she had finished reading the book and said we should share it with others.

So we set out to make that happen. Here it is—the gift to my wife—a story she wanted told.

Our simple wish is that you and your family enjoy this book and know that Danny was right, Christmas doesn't have to end on December 25. Despite disappointments and setbacks that happen to all of us, there is still hope the spirit of the season like fond memories can live on.

Chapter 1

Peter Sampson glanced at his gold rolex. It was 5:25 p.m. He usually pushed it, but this time it looked like he would pay. There was no way he was going to make his flight.

"How much longer?" he asked the limo driver.

"The traffic has been bad sir, but I think I can make it in 15 minutes."

Pete shook his head. His flight was scheduled to leave at 5:35.

He hated waiting in airports. It was such a waste of time. Pete never arrived early for a flight, and he usually got away with it, but it was just three weeks before Christmas and holiday travelers packed LAX—Los Angeles International Airport.

"Would you call the airline to find the status of my flight?" Pete said.

"Certainly sir."

Pete was in a good mood. He had just finished meeting with the district managers of the Southern California-area stores. Sales were up! Not only up, sales were up 16 percent over last year and last year's sales were up 8 percent from the previous year.

Someone was doing something right. If Pete had another hand he'd use it to reach out and pat himself on the back.

The thought of the success of Sampson's Department

Stores made Pete smile every time he thought about it. Christmas was the hap-happiest time of the year.

"Great news Mr. Sampson, your flight has been delayed a half hour. It looks like you'll have time to make it sir."

Pete smiled to himself. It was turning out to be his day. But then again every day was his day.

He had the golden touch.

Last year there was a debate in the company that centered around a major decision—what to do with 13 stores that were losing money. What to do? Close the doors or keep pumping money into them hoping the stores would eventually turn a profit.

Pete lobbied for the stores to remain open and got his way. He spent the next two months in the stores hopping from one community to the other. He studied the competition. One time he stood outside a competitor's store with a clipboard and conducted his own survey.

"Excuse me. Can you tell me why you shop here? Have you ever shopped Sampson's? Why not?"

He then handed them a $20 gift certificate to Sampson's in appreciation for participating in the survey.

Pete knew, by economic studies that had been done, when someone is given a $20 gift certificate, an incredible 87 percent of the people spend more than their gift certificate is worth and 45 percent spend twice the amount of what their certificate is for.

He knew the way to change shoppers' habits was first to get them in his store.

It worked. In just 16 months all but one of the stores that were put on death row were making money and the lone loser was projecting a profit in six months.

The Golden Touch.

"Here we are Mr. Sampson," the driver said.

He opened his door and grabbed his luggage. Pete handed him a $20 bill along with a tiny Christmas card that was slightly bigger than a business card.

"Merry Christmas from Sampson's—your neighbor's

store. Use this certificate to receive 50 percent off any regular-priced item through December."

Pete handed out those cards whenever he could.

At the Western Sky Air terminal, a man held the hand of a young boy and waited in line at the counter for some attention.

It took 15 minutes, but finally he moved his way up to the front of the counter.

"Miss," the man said. "Can I ask your help with my boy. He's only seven and he'll be flying alone. His mother will be picking him up in Chicago. His first flight was coming out to see me. This is only the second time he's been on an airplane. So he'll probably be a little scared."

The lady at the counter was nodding as she punched numbers on her keyboard and stared at the computer screen.

"I'd planned on staying until he boarded, but since the flight was delayed I can't wait. I'm starting my first day at a new job and I've got training..."

The lady finally spoke, cutting the man off.

"Sir, we'll make sure he gets on okay. Next please," she said shewing him away.

The man glanced at her name tag. "Thanks Monica," he said as he put his arm around his boy and walked away. He looked at his watch nervously.

"I've talked to this lady. Her name is Monica. She said she'll take care of you. I wish I could stay with you, but I promised my new job that I would be there for training and I can't be late. I really need this job."

The boy nodded. "I'll be okay dad."

"Give me a squeezer," the man said.

The two embraced for 15 seconds. It was obvious to those in line watching, the man didn't want to leave.

Finally, he let go.

"Okay, give me the best pal handshake."

The boy gave the man a low five, then slipped his hand to the end of the man's hand and locked fingers.

"Woo, woo, woo," they said in unison. "They did the same with the other hand. "Woo, woo, woo."

Then they patted each other on the back in one short embrace. He then kissed the boy and said, "Love ya."

"Love you too, Dad," the boy said.

"I've got to go. I'll call you when you get home. Remember, don't open the present 'till Christmas."

"Daaad," the boy complained. "Okay, I won't," the boy giggled.

He walked up to the counter and interrupted Monica's conversation. "My boy Danny's right there. Don't forget about him. Make sure he gets on okay."

She nodded and waved off the man.

Danny watched his father weave through a herd of travelers until he disappeared from sight.

Suddenly he felt so alone. He swallowed, hoping the lump in his throat would go away, but it didn't. He felt his eyes beginning to water. He struggled to hold back the tears. He didn't want to cry in front of all these strange people.

Pete arrived at the terminal just in time to hear, "Welcome to Western Sky Air. We apologize for the delay, we're ready to board flight 1392 to Chicago. Thank you for your patience. We'd like to ask our First Class passengers to board at this time. Also, children traveling alone and other passengers who need special assistance in boarding."

Pete was carrying a soft leather briefcase. A long business coat covered up his Armani suit. He knew the weather was nice in LA, but once he got to Chicago, he'd be freezing again.

Pete was 42 years old. His brown hair was slicked back with a touch of gray on the sides that gave him a distinguished look. He was just 5'10", 180 pounds, but he carried an awe about him that said, "Don't mess with me."

He was often told he looked like Michael Douglas, a comment that always pleased him.

Despite his size, he looked like a powerful man. He had

hazel eyes and a cheerful disposition that could quickly turn to a scowl. He took off his coat and handed it to a stewardess. He sat down in his usual seat, row eight, the last row to the right in First Class. He liked the window seat. He'd often look down over the world as he flew and come up with some of his best business ideas when he was 30,000 feet over his customers.

He thought of the store's slogan on a round-trip flight from Dallas to Chicago, "Sampson's—we're your neighbor's store."

He wore an "I love Christmas" pin on his suit and today had on a Christmas tie. He was in a festive mood and wanted to share it with everyone.

It was no surprise the flight was full. What few seats that were not booked were quickly filled in with standbys. Pete had actually bought two First Class tickets. Seat A and Seat B, the window and the aisle. He often did this. He didn't like to be crowded.

Sometimes he'd spread out his reports, fire up his laptop computer and do some work on the flight. By booking the seat next to him, Pete guaranteed who'd sit next to him.

Occasionally he liked to talk shop and would invite someone to sit by him. Or he'd strike up a conversation with one of the stewardesses and coax them to sit by him for a rare in-flight break.

All the passengers had boarded except one. The woman with the microphone noticed a boy by himself. Monica's shift ended and in the transition, the seven year-old boy was lost in the crowd. He was nervously clutching his ticket.

"Do you have a ticket for this flight?" the woman asked.

The boy just held out his ticket.

"Why didn't you," she started to say, but she knew the answer to her own question. He didn't know what he was doing. He was traveling by himself and was petrified.

There was a problem now. His seat had already been given to a standby passenger. Pulling someone off a flight was never a pleasant situation, even if they were standbys.

"Follow me," she said to the boy and took his hand.

She walked down the ramp to the plane and explained the situation to Gina, the head stewardess.

Gina's heart skipped a beat and then another when she looked at the boy. His brown hair was shaved on the sides and left longer on top. He had on jeans, a long-sleeved green shirt, and his red jacket was unzipped. He carried a backpack and a fanny pack.

His light complexion highlighted his cheeks like someone had put a touch of blush on them. His long eyelashes would make any woman jealous.

He was the spitting image of Travis, Gina's only son who was five years old. He was just how Gina pictured Travis to look in a few years.

There was only one seat left on the airplane. It was the First-Class seat next to Pete Sampson.

Pete already had his papers out and put his briefcase in the seat. He didn't want anyone thinking this prime seat on the aisle was free.

Gina called two other stewardesses together for a conference. Should they pull off a passenger? They couldn't let the boy wait. Besides, he had a ticket.

Gina decided to ask Pete if he would give up his seat to the boy.

"Mr. Sampson, we have a small problem. We're a seat short. Could we ask you if you would be willing to let one of our young passengers take this seat?"

"I paid for this seat. I need it to do some work. I'm sorry, but I'd say you're out of luck."

Of all the nerve. He didn't want some kid whining by him for three-and-a-half hours. Pete hadn't married for a good reason. Kids were great. They made Christmas what it was, but the only thing he despised more than hearing crying kids on an airplane was going to a movie or a restaurant and having to hear their constant whining outbursts.

"Has anyone every heard of a babysitter?" he often wondered.

As Gina turned around with the boy and headed back toward the cockpit Pete felt guilt creep in. The kid wasn't likely to cry. After all, he was no baby.

"Gina," Pete called out and motioned for her to come back.

He whispered something in her ear and handed her a stack of business cards.

Gina smiled as Pete moved his things off the seat.

The boy sat down, clutching his backpack as if he were afraid Pete would steal it.

Gina would take care of him. She would make sure he wasn't a bother to Mr. Sampson.

The boy looked at Pete's "I love Christmas" pin and smiled.

The excitement of Christmas couldn't be hid in his shy personality.

Gina went through the usual routine of safety procedures in the airplane—how to buckle the seat belt and pull down the oxygen mask.

She had the boy's attention, even though she knew he didn't comprehend a word she'd said.

When Gina finished giving the pre-flight instructions, she checked the boy's seat belt and brought him a small package of cookies, along with a coloring book and crayons. His smile made her homesick.

She leaned over and whispered, "What's your name."

He whispered back, "Danny."

As the plane taxied down the runway and began to pick up speed, Danny closed his eyes as he would on a scary ride at an amusement park.

The plane climbed rapidly and just when it began making its steepest climb, he peeked out of one eye to see a smiling Gina wink at him.

Once the plane reached its cruising altitude of 35,000 feet, Captain Chip Valgardson welcomed the passengers aboard. The weather reports in Chicago were bad, so he figured he'd skip that part. Does anyone really want to know that a storm just dropped 10 inches of snow on the ground and the wind chill is -5 chilling degrees?

While the other flight attendants began the beverage service, Gina delivered a message.

"May I have your attention please. We have a special passenger on board today. We're very pleased to have Mr. Peter Sampson, President and CEO of Sampson Department Stores flying with us.

"Mr. Sampson has asked that I pass out Christmas cards which entitle you to 50 percent off during the month of December as a gift to you. We thank Mr. Sampson for flying Western Sky Air and we thank you all."

There was a small smattering of applause, followed by a short-lived chant, "Pete, Pete, Pete," that was coming from a highschool choir group that numbered 22, including four advisors. They were keeping the back of the plane lively with their laughter and by constantly changing seats with each other. "We know you have other choices," Gina continued. "Let us know if there's anything we can do to make your flight more enjoyable."

Passing out business cards was part of the deal Pete made with Gina when he agreed to give up his seat. Pete smiled to himself as he heard the announcement.

The Golden Touch strikes again. He still had it. Who else would have worked out a way to plug a business on the airline P.A. system?

As Gina started loading drinks on her cart, she felt relieved. Some flights that were four hours felt like twelve. Others seemed like just when they were reaching cruising altitude, they started their descent.

Having Mr. Sampson give Danny his seat was a huge relief. She was getting a kick out of how well Danny was getting along with Mr. Sampson.

Her experience told her this flight would fly by. Having logged over 1,000 flights in her six years as a stewardess had eased her fear of flying.

This was the fun part—interacting with people. Even

though the plane was full, passengers were always in a good mood around the holidays and much more patient, providing there were no delays.

But within five minutes all that would change.

Chapter 2

It suddenly occurred to Pete that he had a great resource sitting next to him. Who better to find out what toys were hot this year than a seven year old?

He seemed like an average kid. What commercials would he remember? Pete thought it would be fascinating to pick his brain and see what Christmas campaigns were working.

Pete could find out what kind of toys the boy had and how many of them Sampson's carried. He could find out where his family shopped and why. Another great idea, if Pete did say so himself.

The boy hadn't said a word and the plane had been airborn for 30 minutes. He took a glance at the boy who was quietly coloring in the color book Gina, the stewardess, had given him.

Pete looked down at the coloring book. "Nice picture, son. What's your name?"

The boy looked up and said his name but all Pete could hear was "knee."

He didn't bother asking him again.

"So how old are you?"

"Seven," he said without looking up.

Pete wondered who would let a seven year old travel from LA to Chicago by himself.

Pete planned on spending most of the flight going over

some reports, but he didn't feel like it now. He was too excited about his new idea.

Danny's picture was beginning to take shape. It was a picture of Santa Claus in his sleigh dropping presents out of the sky.

The presents were colored with great care and detail. It was pretty good—for a boy his age, it was remarkable.

Danny could feel the excitement of Christmas building as he was coloring the picture.

"Wow, that's a great picture Danny," Gina said as she kneeled over and took the empty cookie wrapper. "Do you need something to drink?"

He nodded.

"Do you want juice or Sprite?"

"Sprite please."

Gina poured him half a cup and finished serving drinks to the rest of the passengers in first class.

"So have you told Santa what you want for Christmas," Pete asked.

Danny looked up with a smile. "I got my present already. I got to come and see my dad."

Then he began fumbling in his fanny pack and pulled out a small box that was wrapped in Christmas green colored paper, with a red ribbon. He proudly showed Pete.

"Wow! Ooh, that looks like a super deluxe present," Pete said with excitement.

He then whispered to Danny. "Do you know what it is?"

Danny whispered back, "No," as he shook the box. "Do you?" Danny asked with a wide-eyed excitement.

"Can I hold it?" Pete asked.

Danny nodded and carefully handed him the present like he was giving him a full glass of milk that he was trying not to spill.

Pete pressed it gently and held it up to his ear. He gave Danny a curious look like he was in a taste test and someone was waiting for his approval.

"Humm. It could be..."

Danny scooted up in his seat. "Nah."

Danny's facial expression sank. "Or it could be..."

Danny was excited again.

"I just don't know. I think you'll have to wait until Christmas to find out."

"Oh," Danny said in a disappointing tone. "I can't wait until Christmas."

Pete handed Danny the gift back. Danny carefully put it back in his fanny pack, barely getting the zipper closed.

Danny returned to his picture. It was almost done. He was starting to feel comfortable with Pete. Enough so that he mustered up the courage to ask him for a piece of paper.

"Hey, mister. Do you have a piece of paper I could have please?"

"Sure, you drawing another picture?"

"Nope. I'm writing Santa a letter to go with this picture."

"So were you just out here visiting your father?" Pete asked.

"Yeah. My mom said I could come and see him. I haven't seen him since I was six. He moved away," Danny said, his tongue sticking out of the side of his mouth like he was Michael Jordan driving to the basket, while he colored Santa's boots black.

"So what did you do in California? Did you go to Disneyland? Or Sea World?"

"No, my dad said he would take me next time. But he had lots of time to spend with me. We went to the beach a lot, but it was too cold to do much. He said he'd show me how to body surf when I come out again next summer. My dad's lucky. He never has to go to work."

Pete sat back in his seat. The picture of Danny's life was taking shape. The different colors were now visible.

Chapter 3

Tina McMurtrey looked up at the clock again. She began sliding her notes into her backpack. Class was supposed to end at 7 p.m. and it was 7:03. She had too much to do to stay any longer and listen to more stupid comments from her classmates who had nothing better to do.

Besides, what did algebra have to do with public relations? Tina wanted a job in the Chicago Cubs front office where she was working as an intern. What was she going to do with this math junk? Run an algebraic equation on how many hats would be given away on hat day? That was something for the marketing department to handle.

Tina concluded that taking classes that seem to be worthless is just part of the initiation of getting a bachelor's degree.

Tina had the personality and looks for public relations. She had long brown hair that reached the middle of her back. It looked good and rather professional, smashing the stereotype that women had to have short hair to come across as a professional. Her hair matched her 5-foot-11 inch frame. She rarely did anything different to it. In fact, her looks, along with her hairstyle, seldom changed. She was fortunate to look good with little makeup. People compared her to Demi Moore so often that when they did she'd developed a patented answer.

"Thanks, I got her looks, now if I could only have her

money."

Tina planned on stopping by Peppermint Place candy store to pick up two pounds of fudge, a rare delicacy for Danny. He loved fudge more than sleeping in on Saturday morning and waking up to the smell of sizzling bacon. He loved it so much Tina seldom made it for him or bought any because he ate it so fast, he inevitably got sick. It would make the perfect surprise.

Even though Danny had only been gone a week, it seemed like a year plus interest. For Tina, one week without Danny was like she was serving a prison sentence behind bars. She wanted Danny home and couldn't wait another hour. She was as impatient as a fire engine following a car that won't pull over.

Tina found shopping for Danny helped her miss him a little less. Besides, she wanted to finish up all her Christmas shopping by Dec. 7, the day Danny came back.

To be done so early would be a record, but it fit in with her goal of spending more time with Danny. Of course, this year she could finish in one night. She could finish in one store, with one purchase.

Credit and her mixed like Santa and a plate of carrot sticks. That's what a divorce will do for you.

After her divorce a year and a half ago, Tina decided to finish the degree she started seven years ago. She hadn't planned on going to school, but her husband Rick showed no interest in getting a degree, so she went. She felt like someone in the family should have one.

The honeymoon lasted no longer than two months. With a baby on the way, and no health insurance, Tina was forced to put her school on the bookshelf and become a working mother after just one semester.

After their divorce, Rick, who still didn't know what he wanted to do with his life, moved to Naperville, Illinois, 45 minutes south of Chicago.

Tina stayed in Evanston, 10 to 15 minutes north of Chicago. To go from Naperville to Evanston took anywhere from an hour to an hour and a half, depending on traffic.

Rick and Tina had their irreconcilable differences. Tina would often repeat what she'd now come to believe; Rick was the most irresponsible person she'd ever met. That's why she had always been quite surprised by the attention and love Rick had always shown Danny. She couldn't figure out how Danny got Rick to love him in a way she never could. There must be some kind of instinctive bond, a father-and-son thing she figured.

Even though it was hard to see Rick so often, she was grateful their divorce had been amicable. They had a boy together and nothing could change that. Despite the hurt and anger she felt toward Rick, she was determined to never say anything negative about him to Danny and she never had, despite the fact that she'd only received one check for child support. The check was only $200, only about half what she was supposed to get.

Rick's indecision about his future was wrecking his present. He had hopped from job to job for the last three years.

His longest stint was actually at a pet store. He loved reptiles. It seemed to be a perfect fit, but 14 months later, he was fired when someone brought in an Iguana they no longer wanted. Rick took a liking to it and took it home instead of putting it in as inventory and offering it for resale.

When his brother from Anaheim called with a job offer with a start-up company, the only hesitation he had was Danny.

But unemployed and with no prospects in sight, he went.

Tina returned her attention to the doodle she'd been working on in class. It was the blueprint of a Christmas card she planned on making. She had already cut out pictures of Sammy Sosa from three different magazines that would fit neatly inside the card.

But there was a problem. She couldn't decide what type

of lettering to use on the outside of the card. Should she go with Merry Christmas? Or would Merry Christmas look better?

Actually, she doubted he would care, as long as there was a picture of Sammy Sosa on the card. She could make it look like it was from Sammy himself. Maybe she'd send it to her own address and pretend it was from Wrigley Field. She could use Cubs stationary.

Is that wrong she wondered?

Tina had it all planned. When Danny arrived, they'd stop by the Shake Factory on the way home from the airport. What a funny kid Danny was. He liked ice cream more in the winter than the summer. This time he could get the jumbo with Oreos and Butterfingers. Heck, throw anything chocolate in there—the gooier the better.

Humm, she just might have to help him eat some.

In the morning they would put up their Christmas tree. Even though it always ended up in two or three blobs, she would let Danny put on the tinsel, his favorite part. He just liked throwing it on the tree. Last year Tina tried to even it out to make it look good, but Danny looked on with hurtful eyes.

"Don't you like it mom?"

"Yeah, come to think of it, I like it just the way it is. I'd never change a thing."

Then they would pop popcorn and use it as decoration for the tree.

Danny had already made a green and red paper chain that was taped to the side of the refrigerator, waiting to be put on the tree.

Tina wanted to be at the airport at least 30 minutes early. She would be taking no chances. It was Danny's first trip on an airplane. She was a nervous wreck when he left for California and now the nerves returned.

She didn't want him wandering around the airport by himself.

"See you next week," the instructor said, snapping her

out of her daydream.

"Finally," Tina mumbled as she scooted down the aisle. While the other students put their books away, she was already walking toward the door.

Tina figured she'd stop at one store on the way to the airport anyway, since she knew she wouldn't be coming out this way again before Christmas.

The only means she had for shopping was her credit card. There was only a $2,000 limit on the card and unfortunately she'd used $1,973 of it. She could easily be done shopping after getting one present. But just one present for Christmas? She shook her head at the thought.

Tina had $27 left on her credit card, and she still hadn't found the perfect present.

She pulled into the South Town mall and drove in circles looking for a parking spot. Finally she settled for one by a bus stop in the overflow parking section.

"This is ridiculous," she thought as she wrapped her scarf around her neck and made the long walk to the mall. "There ought to be a shuttle if you park this far out."

She sidestepped through the crowds, pausing at one store, going in another. Ah, Peppermint Place. She bought two pounds of fudge—ouch, $12.

Only time for one more stop. She went in Christmas Creations. Her eyes went right to it—a snow globe. She picked it up. It had several little children ice skating around a rink. In the middle of the rink was a big chair where Santa sat holding a boy in his lap.

Santa's face was big enough to see a smile. The boy had an expression of excitement that only Christmas could exact.

The globe was bigger than most; about the size of a large head of lettuce. Tina picked it up and held it close so she could see in the globe. Then she turned it upside down and watched the snowflakes fall. Perfect.

Danny would love it. She knew how he loved Christmas. It would remind him of Christmas all year long and give him something to look forward to.

She turned the price tag over—$34. Maybe she was wrong on her credit card balance. She hoped.

The clerk gave her an uneasy look. She didn't have to say anything. In fact, before she could, Tina dug into her purse and pulled out her checkbook.

She knew she was bouncing a check. Another $15 charged to her account. It wasn't the first.

She had it gift wrapped in forest green paper with a gold bow.

Tina was now in a good mood. She scurried out the door. There was no way she was going to be late for Danny's flight.

Danny was starting to feel at ease with Pete. He held up one of his pictures for approval. Pete stared at it, held it close to his eyes, then held up a finger as if to say, "Wait."

He pulled out his glasses for a closer look. A smile surfaced. "Ah, this is very good. In fact, this is exceptional.

"Who is this for? Is it for sale? How much do you want for it? I like to buy paintings. I'd like to buy this one."

Danny giggled.

"I'm not selling these. They're just drawings."

"I know but they're very good. Do you draw in school?"

Danny nodded eagerly.

"I just want you to have it," Danny said. He'd already gotten out a new piece of paper to start another picture.

Peter pulled out his wallet and gave Danny a $10 bill.

But he didn't seem remotely interested in the money.

"Nah, it's free," he said bashfully. "Merry Christmas."

Pete peered out the window. It was just getting dark. He stared at the white peaks on the distant mountains.

As he settled back in his seat, a loud boom rang throughout from the rear of the plane. Pete jumped in his seat, a reflex reaction like someone had just hit his knee with a hammer. It shook the plane with a quick and powerful jolt.

Pete sat up straight in his seat as he felt the plane start

to lose altitude like it was beginning its descent.

What happened? A few faint screams from coach rang out. A woman across the aisle sounded like she was hyperventilating.

Danny grabbed the arm rest like he was holding onto the safety bar on a roller coaster. He looked up at Pete with the expression a child looks at its parents when waking up from a bad dream.

Pete's first thought was that they had grazed another plane. In fact he looked out the window again thinking he might be able to see the other plane. He dismissed the collision theory, based on the fact that they were already at cruising altitude and they were still flying.

Maybe it was a bomb. Someone in coach was a wacko. That wouldn't surprise him. He watched several passengers walk by when they boarded and already had a handful of suspects.

He put his hand on Danny's and looked for Gina. Something was definitely wrong. Everyone on the plane knew it. After a few seconds of quiet terror, passengers were beginning to shout out questions to the flight attendants.

"Air traffic control, this is Sky West Flight 1392. We have a problem," Captain Valgardson said.

Finally, the captain got on the P.A. system. It was only a minute and a half after the explosion, but it felt like an hour of uncertainty had passed. Captain Valgardson wanted to wait until he knew more, but he also knew if he didn't say something soon, the passengers could riot with panic. It could get ugly, and quick.

"May I have your attention please."

Chapter 4

It was deathly quiet inside the plane. It was like being in a cave all by yourself. You could hear water drip off a stalactite into a pool of water.

There was a slight pause followed by a shaking of the cabin that filled the plane with screams again.

Tears began forming in Danny's eyes.

"Please remain clam," the captain said. "We've had a problem with one of our engines."

A series of cries and "Ohs" ran up and down the aisle like a wave.

"But I can assure you this plane is very capable of flying with two engines. We will be making an unscheduled stop in Salt Lake City to have the plane checked, but I can assure you this aircraft will fly with two engines without any difficulty. We apologize for this inconvenience."

What the captain left out was that the rear of the plane had been damaged and he had already felt a significant loss in ability to fly the plane.

Gina was kneeling down holding the hand of the lady behind Pete on the other side of First Class. The lady was just now starting to calm down.

Pete could still hear some sobs and crying. A baby who had started screaming when her mother did, began to quiet down. A sense of temporary relief spread throughout the plane.

Pete returned his attention to Danny. Incredibly, Danny was now calm. In fact, when Pete looked down he noticed Danny had finished his picture and written some kind of message to Santa on the back of his drawing. He couldn't tell what it was before Danny folded up the drawing and carefully licked an envelope and sealed it closed, rubbing the back of it like he was giving someone a massage.

This was one letter he wanted to make sure made it to its destination.

"To Sanda Klaws," was written in red crayon on the front of the envelope.

On the next line Danny had written the address "The North Pol."

The only word that was written in the the upper left hand corner of the envelope was Danny. No last name. No return address. Just Danny, as if Santa would know.

He then slipped it into his backpack, determined to put it in the first mailbox he found.

Gina spent the next five minutes calming the fears of passengers, answering questions as if she were the pilot. She reassured the panicked that the plane wasn't going to crash.

After she'd put on her best impression trying to convince herself, she walked toward the cockpit, her eyes misty, fighting to hold back her tears along with her fear.

The plane vibrated as it banked to turn. Something was not right. Gina needed to know how bad the situation was.

She paused with shock as she reached the door of the cockpit and heard the warning bell going off on the instrument panel.

"Captain, the warning light on Engine No. 2 is on," Paul Cuff, the First Officer said.

Captain Valgardson looked at the instrument panel. The red light was a warning to tell the pilot to look at the engine performance instruments.

The RPM gauge was dropping rapidly. The EPR gauge was also falling and the oil pressure was zero.

The RPM and EPR indications meant one thing: low

thrust. In laymen's terms, the engine was shot. It was worthless.

But the engine was the last of the crew's worries. More alarming was the fact that a yellow caution light started to flash. The hydraulic fluid was low.

Captain Valgardson decided to turn the plane to check what control he had of it. His eyebrows formed a scowl.

The controls were sluggish. Just as he thought. He looked back down at all three gauges. All readings were just barely above zero.

With no hydraulics to steer the plane, the captain began to offer a small prayer.

"Please God help me. Help me use my experience and knowledge to save these people. There are children. God help me save them."

Gina finally knocked on the door. "Yes," Captain Valgardson said in an irritated tone.

"I'm sorry, captain."

"Please begin to prepare the passengers for an emergency landing," the captain said.

"I'll give everyone an update."

Gina slowly shut the door.

"Wait. Gina."

She opened the door.

Gina didn't know much about the mechanics of an airplane but she did know the plane could fly with two of the three engines.

Before she could ask what else was wrong, the captain added, "There may be another problem."

Captain Valgardson looked down to find the fire light was on. The bum engine was now on fire.

"We're having some trouble controlling the plane. It's just not responding very well. Try and keep them busy," he said. "We're going to try and land in Salt Lake."

Gina turned around, her heart beating like a bass drum at a rock concert.

Try and land in Salt Lake? He said *try*, *not we will be*

landing in Salt Lake.

Her first thought. Her only thought was "My Travis. I can't die. What will he do? Who will take care of him? He needs me."

She wiped the tears from her face and as she reappeared from the cockpit, she pretended to be doing something at the flight attendant's station, while she frantically tried to compose herself. Gina knew no passengers could see her fear. She had to be strong.

Of all the difficult jobs in the world, what could be more challenging than being a flight attendant on a plane in trouble?

Sharell, another flight attendant, came up from behind her and put her arm on her shoulder. "You okay?"

"Yeah," she said with a sniffle. "How are they in your section?"

"They're pretty nervous. They keep asking questions like, 'What's the vibration? Is that normal?'"

Gina smiled. She felt a sense of renewed strength. Sharell was a comfort. Funny, it was Gina, the Head Flight Attendant, who was supposed to be the one calm, cool and collected.

She gave Sharell a hug. "Can you get the others up front? The captain has asked us to prepare the passengers for an emergency landing. We're going to be landing at Salt Lake City airport."

Sharell looked surprised. Maybe she underestimated the seriousness of the situation, but she smiled and said, "I'll be right back."

The crew, Captain Valgardson, First Officer Paul Cuff and Second Officer Chad Toliver immediately went through the checklist. First, Valgardson moved the throttle to "off." He then discharged the fire retardant into the engine bay to extinguish the fire in the No. 2 engine bay.

Meanwhile, Cuff looked for smoke. Nothing. There were no other indications other than the warning lights.

While Gina was prepping the passengers, Captain

Valgardson determined, through air traffic control, that Salt Lake City would be a better option than Las Vegas.

"Salt Lake City, this is Western Sky Air 1392," Valgardson said. "We're having trouble controlling this bird."

Paul looked over at the captain with a shocked expression.

"We can't turn left."

"What? We can't turn left?" Toliver said in a panicked tone.

"We've lost our hydraulics," the captain told the crew.

"Salt Lake, this is Western Sky Air 1392. We've blown the No. 2 engine. We've lost all hydraulics and we can only maneuver using asymmetrical power settings, which means the only way to turn the airplane is to vary the thrust on the engines."

Toliver rested his head back on his seat.

His first thought was, "So this is how it all ends." The great mystery of life ends in my 42nd year. Three children and an ex-wife.

It's funny the things that you think about when you know you're going to die.

"I wonder if Janet would come to my funeral if it weren't for the kids," he thought.

A thousand other thoughts began racing through Toliver's mind. His eighth birthday party at a Wisconsin park. All he could remember about it was the cake had chocolate frosting with a three-inch candy baseball bat on top of it.

All his thoughts somehow went back to his childhood.

There was the time he climbed a small maple tree to peak into a nest of a Robin, but his weight on the branch caused the nest to tumble from the tree. There were five baby birds; three were chirping, the other two lay motionless on the ground. Another bird, the mother, screeched from a distance.

It was a feeling of helplessness. It's exactly how he now felt.

Chapter 5

Captain Valgardson was slow to panic. He'd had a number of close calls in his 24 years of flying 737s, 747s and DC 10s, the model now giving him so much trouble.

There was a near miss one time when he was flying up the coast of central California. He was flying about 15,000 feet when suddenly the TCAS warning system went off, indicating another plane was getting dangerously close.

"TRAFFIC, TRAFFIC."

He looked inside the TCAS display and saw a target at 12 o'clock and five miles away. He looked out the window but couldn't see anything. The co-pilot queried the ATC if there was a plane.

The TCAS went off again and this time the computerized warning voice said, "TRAFFIC, PULL UP."

Captain Valgardson again looked at the TCAS display. He felt a chill run up his spine. The target was now in red at close range. He immediately began to climb. He looked out the window and saw a small Cesna 310 zipping under the nose of the plane.

It took Captain Valgardson a good 20 minutes for his heartbeat to return to normal. Had he not started his climb, he knew the Cesna would have smashed into his 737 and both of them would have gone down.

One time he was flying a plane that had trouble with the landing gear. When Captain Valgardson switched down the landing gear, the right main gear light remained red, indicating the landing gear was not locked and in position.

The crew quickly went through their checklist. Their worry was they would run out of fuel before they could get the landing gear down. One of the flight crew went out into the cabin to look through the viewing window to check the position of the right main gear. Sure enough, the landing gear wasn't down.

The crew manually pulled the gear release in the cockpit and managed to avoid a potentially disastrous situation by getting the landing gear down.

Then there was the time he had an engine fail, but that time he had little trouble with the plane. In fact, they continued on with their flight from Denver and landed in Dallas without having to make an unscheduled stop.

Every close call had turned out the same—safe. The experiences left Captain Valgardson with a calm and steady hand.

But this topped them all. Before, he never had time to panic. Instinct kicked in and he was forced to rely on his experience before he even had time to think about it.

This was different. For the first time in his career, he wondered if his number was up. He actually thought there may be nothing he could do. But the captain wouldn't let those negative thoughts last long.

He may have just been dealt a lousy hand in poker, but he still appeared poised and confident that he wouldn't fold.

What worried the captain the most was the sluggishness of the controls. It was like trying to steer a car with the engine off.

"Western Sky Air 1392. This is Salt Lake City. Fly heading two four zero and tell me souls on board."

There was no response from flight 1392.

Finally, after a long pause, the captain responded with, "We've lost all hydraulics. All hydraulic systems are lost."

Stewart Sinclair was specifically trained for emergency situations like this. He was now looking over the shoulder of

Preston Walker, who was handling the contact with Flight 1392.

Preston slammed his fist on the counter.

Stewart turned to the men in the tower and said, “Get emergency crews standing by. Alert the surrounding counties. It will be an act of God if he makes the runway.”

“Western Sky 1392, please give me souls on board.”

The crew knew the tower needed a definite number, but it was like the vultures were already circling. It was just another reminder of the trouble they were in.

“We’re working on it,” Cuff responded in a testy tone.

There were still other things to check out.

“What is the status of engines one and three?” Stewart said.

“We have normal engine power on one and three,” the captain said.

The tower chipped back in.

“Western Sky 1392, state souls on board and remaining fuel.”

Chapter 6

Rick Bailey was stuck in traffic, he had been flipped off twice and was going to be late for a training session at work, but he still had a smile on his face.

Life was good. It had only been a few months since he moved to LA from Chicago and the job his brother promised him hadn't materialized. He was still sleeping on the floor of his brother's apartment because the couch was too small, but for the first time he could see a future for himself and for Danny.

Rick's brother Ben often told him to be patient, that delays are not unusual with start-up companies. Rick had little room to complain. He really had no other options and he was living off Ben. He had no money to send for child support, but he rationalized that he would make up for it once he got rich with this new company.

Rick was to be at work for a two-hour training session with three other employees. The starting pay was just $12.50 an hour, but Ben convinced Rick that when the company took off he'd move up with it.

It was the beginning of California Price Savers Club—get everything at wholesale. For a $50 yearly membership fee, the CPS Club, as it was being marketed, would guarantee the lowest prices on the items that they offered.

Of course not all brands were available, but Ben and his partner Darin, who financed the project, were sold on the idea. Sure there were plenty of other wholesale companies, especially on the Internet, but they offered such a variety—from bulk food items to airline tickets, from tires to blue jeans. The kicker was they would deliver right to your door (within a certain area).

Darin and Ben were banking on the belief that people would pay for the convenience.

Rick had no idea what he would be doing, he just knew he was supposed to be at the office at 6:00 p.m. It was now 6:15 and the way the traffic was moving, he'd be another 30 minutes.

He knew Ben was going to be furious, but instead of worrying about it, he kept thinking of Danny. In the few days that Danny had come out to visit, Rick embraced him as part of his lonely life. He was excited for the prospects of bringing Danny back in April when he could fly him out and take him to Disneyland and Universal Studios. He'd take Danny to the beach and teach him how to body surf.

Rick came to a complete stop. He sighed and looked down at his key chain. He had a picture taken with Danny at one of the souvenir shops. They put the picture inside the key chain. One for Danny and one for dad.

Rick laughed and then said out loud, "That cute little Tyke, I just love him."

A horn honked and snapped Rick's attention back to the road.

"We're not going to make the runway," the captain said to himself and the rest of the crew.

Optimism had now taken a back seat to realism.

"We have no hydraulic fluid which means we have no elevator control and little aileron control," the captain told Salt Lake Tower. "Have you got someplace nearby that we can ditch this bird? Unless we get a miracle from God and we're able to get control of this thing, we're going to put it down wherever it happens to be and I prefer the alternative."

"Western Sky Air 1392, have you lost all manual flight

control systems?" Stewart asked.

"Affirmative."

The captain closed his eyes tight as he thought about their fate for a split second. "There must be some way out of this. Think, think. Over 300 people are counting on me."

After a long silent pause, the captain got back on the radio.

"Maybe we'll set it down in the Great Salt Lake. I hear everything floats in that lake," he said, trying to take some pressure off the situation.

The plane continued to make right turns and was now down to 15,000 feet.

But as the crew got closer to Salt Lake International, the circles had scrambled their sense of direction.

"Just keep us away from the city," the captain told the tower.

Captain Valgardson knew what he had to do. The passengers had the right to know the situation. They needed to be ready for a rough landing and to make peace with God, he thought.

"May I have your attention please," the captain said.

"Please give the flight attendants your full cooperation. We will be landing in Salt Lake shortly.

"We're going to ask you to prepare for an emergency landing. We believe some damage has been done to our rudders and it's making the plane a little more tricky to control.

"We'll get through this though. Just follow the instructions you're given and listen carefully."

After a slight pause to quell the emotions, the captain said simply, "Thank you."

Gina and the other flight attendants gave emergency landing instructions. Passengers were told to place their heads between their legs at the point of impact.

Gina would lead the instructions with, "Brace. Brace."

That meant impact would be just 20 seconds away.

Pete looked around the First Class section. A retired couple gripped each others' hands tightly. She was on the aisle. A few tears escaped from behind her dark glasses and down her face.

Danny had grown quiet, but still didn't seem too bothered by the commotion. After the captain spoke for the first time, he was calm. His fears had walked out on the wing and blown away.

Gina was too busy to be scared now. But she was determined to take 30 seconds for herself. She had to let her son know, in possibly her last hours, that all her thoughts were with him.

"Please, whoever finds this note, give it to my son Travis at 1455 Seal Beach Drive. Long Beach, California.

> Dear Travis:
>
> The next part was hard to read. Tears had smudged the ink.
>
> "You know I love you, sweetie. Remember the movie ET? Remember how his heart glowed inside when he loved someone? That's how I feel about you. My heart glows for you right now. It always has and always will. No matter where I am. I will always be thinking of you. Watching over you. Loving you. Don't forget that love is the strongest power in this life. It can even conquer Hulk Hogan.
>
> Goodbye for now. Sometimes you may not know it, but I'll be with you always.
>
> I love you. Mom.

There was so much more Gina wanted to say. But she felt guilty as it was. Here she was writing a letter to her son, thinking of herself and not the passengers who were in her care.

A tremendous shake followed when the plane began banking a turn. Screams cut Gina's letter short.

Chapter 7

The curtains to the First Class section were open. Susie Shumway couldn't help but notice Danny, who seemed to be looking around at where the screams were coming from.

Her heart sank. Poor kid. She heard Gina ask Pete to give up his seat for one of the plane's youngest passengers.

He's all alone. All she could think about was helping him. She wanted to get out of her seat and give him a hug. She wanted to tell him it was going to be okay, but the flight attendants were making no exceptions. No one was to get out of their seats. Period.

So Susie waited until the right time, unbuckled her seat belt and kissed Danny on the check and whispered in his ear.

Gina frowned when she saw her out of her seat and began to open her mouth, but nothing came out. She quickly realized what Susie was trying to do.

"I have an extra piece of bubble gum in my pocket. Let's have a bubble blowing contest," Susie said.

Danny's face beamed with excitement. It was the same look he gave Pete when he talked about Christmas.

He turned back and watched Susie get back into her seat and snap on her seat belt.

Her blue eyes sparkled back at his tender face and her bright smile was like a diamond shining in a cabin filled with gloom and doom and the darkness of death.

Susie may have been from Chicago, but she acted like

she was from California. Since late August, she had spent all her time studying outside. She hated studying in her dorm room.

The beach, a favorite spot on campus—anywhere was better to study in than her room. Besides, she loved people. You couldn't meet anyone locked in your room. As an added bonus, she had gotten a nice tan on her face and on her legs. It was her own personal souvenir she could take back to Chicago, a reminder to everyone back home that she was at UCLA.

Susie was studying finance and secretly studying acting, something her parents discouraged.

The contest started off with a little bubble that popped just after it appeared visible from Susie's lips. But she quickly rebounded by blowing a huge pink bubble that covered most of her face.

She held it for a few seconds. Finally it deflated and spread over her nose and cheeks.

Danny erupted in laughter, which caught the attention of every passenger within the sound of his giggles.

Now it was his turn. Danny huffed and puffed but nothing happened.

He chomped his gum and got it in position, then tried again.

His tongue poked out. A tiny bubble formed and began growing slowly. Big, bigger, bigger.

"Wow," Susie shouted just as his bubble burst.

Danny giggled and began to peel the gum off his nose.

Susie got out another piece of bubble gum. Danny's eyebrows raised as if to say, "No fair."

Susie laughed and tossed it to him.

"Great catch," Susie said.

Suddenly the plane shook violently, snapping Danny's attention back to the crisis at hand.

Pete was writing in his appointment book, exercising the optimism that he'd become famous for when the screams and vibrations stopped his writing.

He slipped his book inside his shirt pocket and turned his attention back to Danny.

"May I have your attention," the captain said. "We'll be landing in a few minutes. It won't be one of my smoothest landings, so please listen carefully. When I say, 'Brace, Brace, Brace,' that means prepare for landing. It should be about 20 seconds before we touch down.

"The flight attendants will be available to help assist you for the next few minutes. Please pay attention to their instructions. Thank you for your cooperation."

Gina took over the P.A. system and reviewed the emergency landing procedures.

"When you hear, 'Brace, Brace, Brace,' that's the sign. Bend over with your head between your knees and with both hands grab the seat in front of you."

The flight attendants had positioned themselves around the aircraft, demonstrating the position.

It was the only time in all her years of talking to the passengers that she had every passenger's undivided attention.

Since there was a chance of landing in water, the flight attendants spent a few minutes on how the seats could be made into a flotation device.

Landing in the Great Salt Lake was unlikely since flight 1392 was flying in from the south and the lake that made Utah famous was just a few miles north (and west) of the SLI runway.

But Utah Lake was a real possibility. Utah Lake is the largest fresh water lake in Utah, covering 139 square miles and it is in the direct flight path of planes flying in from the west.

The one break Flight 1392 had going for it was there were three airports within 40 miles of each other. SLI, Airport No. 2 and the Provo Airport. Airport No. 2 was 15 miles southwest of Salt Lake City and was used mainly for smaller planes . It didn't have a runway long enough for flight 1392, but it was better than a subdivision.

Besides, a field bordered the end of the runway. Since it was so close to Salt Lake International it would be used as a last resort.

If Captain Valgardson couldn't make Salt Lake, the crew would shoot for the Provo Airport, which was surrounded by Utah Lake from all sides except the east.

The runway at Provo was big enough (6,500 feet) but there was a good chance the plane wouldn't be able to use reverse thrusters or its flaps. If that happened, the amount of fuel the plane was carrying, along with the fact that Flight 1392 was packed, made it highly unlikely it would be able to stop in time, slamming into a moat-like river that surrounded the airport.

Provo was also not equipped with the emergency equipment. This had all the makings of a mess. But if Captain Valgardson couldn't make Salt Lake, he was landing in Provo—short runway or not.

Since the plane could only bank to its right, the crew continued to struggle to get its bearings on where they were.

"Just keep me away from the city and the mountains," the captain kept telling the tower.

"Western Sky 1392, if you can't make SLI there is an interstate that runs north to south," the tower said.

Captain Valgardson didn't want any part of an interstate. With so little control of the plane he knew it would be risky trying to set it down on an interstate so close to Salt Lake City. There were too many businesses, malls, schools, and churches nearby.

But he knew he only had a small hand in where the plane would go. He felt as helpless as a driver's education instructor out on the road with a student driver.

"Western Sky 1392, winds are currently three, six, zero, at one, three sixty at eleven. You're clear to land on any runway."

The captain and Cuff looked at each other and laughed.

"How about if we use all of them?" Cuff said.

The passengers were now quiet. Susie was holding the hand of a lady next to her, a middle-aged woman who was having a harder time accepting their fate than most of the other passengers. She was now crying out loud and kept asking questions to whatever flight attendant she could get to listen to her.

Susie reached down in her bag under her seat and pulled out a Kleenex. She wiped the tears off the woman's face, hoping Danny wouldn't hear her emotional breakdown.

The captain rang for Gina one last time. As she walked past Pete, he stopped her and whispered something into her ear.

"Gina, please tell me. Which is the safer seat, the window or the aisle?"

Gina seemed shocked at the question. She wondered for a second if Pete was setting her up to improve his own chances of survival, but as she paused to think about it, she could see he was sincere.

Even though Gina wasn't sure—she'd never been in a situation like this—her guess would be the window seat. She nodded at his seat.

"Thank you," Pete said.

Gina stepped into the cockpit.

"Is everyone ready?" the Captain said.

"Yes. We're prepared for landing."

"It's going to be pretty rough. Say a prayer for us."

Gina put her hand on the captain's shoulder. "I will. Good luck," she said as she blinked furiously trying to conceal her tears.

Gina made one last look over the cabin. The look on the passengers' faces cut her heart. She'd never seen such a sad sight in her life. She knew not all the passengers would survive. She seemed to know this and accept it as a fact. She wondered about their families and what they were doing right now. What they would give to see them one more time.

Which ones would live and which ones would die? She figured less than half would survive, maybe one out of three.

Maybe none of them would make it.

She said a silent prayer to herself as she returned to her seat and strapped her seat belt on. She squeezed the hand of Sharell tightly as they looked at each other, hoping to calm each others' fears, then returned to her prayer.

"God be with them all, your children. Bring peace to their souls in this their final hour. Forgive us of our neglect and bless our loved ones. Bless the captain and our crew and Lord guide their hands if it be thy will that we may live to praise thee. Bless the children that they may not suffer."

She paused, "and bless Danny that he will..." she started to say live, but knew that wouldn't be fair to ask God to save him over other passengers, but her heart gave away her feelings.

"Just bless Danny and keep him in thy hand."

Pete turned to Danny and said, "Why don't you trade me seats? That way you can see out the window."

Danny didn't want to look out the window, but agreed to change after Pete had already taken his seat belt off and was scooting over toward him.

Pete personally put the seat belt on Danny.

"Is that too tight?"

"That's good," Danny said.

Pete cinched it up a bit tighter. He was taking no chances.

Gina returned to her prayer. She had so much to say, but the captain's command cut her prayer short.

"Brace, Brace, Brace."

Chapter 8

Pete had his head down staring at the floor waiting for what he anticipated to be a violent impact.

He could hear Danny crying lightly. He thought he was saying, “Mommy.”

Even though Pete had no children, he’d never felt closer to another child in his life.

It was the single saddest moment of his life. In these final seconds waiting to live or die, he felt like someone had lit a firecracker and the fuse had just disappeared. The firecracker was still smoldering. The anticipation of impact was intense.

Danny had pricked Pete’s heart, and feelings he’d never known before trickled out. His thoughts now centered on Danny. He didn’t want Danny’s last moments to be crying, so he tapped on his shoulder and when he saw Danny’s tear-streaked face, he stuck out his tongue.

Danny laughed. Then Pete put his thumbs to his ears and wiggled his fingers. Danny giggled and laughed out loud again.

BOOM!

The sound of impact rang throughout the cabin. It was like standing within an ear’s length of a freight train that’s just leaving a steel mill, thousands of pounds of metal shifting and now moving forward.

But worse.

Pete gripped the seat in front of him, but upon impact it was like someone was testing his flexes and hitting his knee at the right spot.

He had no control of his hands. They popped off the seat in front of him as his head snapped up.

Pete now opened his eyes, but quickly shut them again. He felt like he was on a rollercoaster going down a huge hill. It was like he had zero gravity. He was floating in air, with just his seat belt keeping him in his seat.

He opened his eyes again hoping the ride was almost over and saw an empty seat fly past him along with all variations of bags and unrecognizable objects.

Pete had never felt so utterly helpless in his life. All his life he believed he could control his fate. He would determine whether he would be rich or poor. He would live to be ninety years old if he chose to. The power of positive thinking could conquer all.

But not this. Now he realized he had no control of his life. He felt like his neck had been placed in a guillotine. He was blindfolded and just waiting for the blade to slam down on him, ending his life.

In the seconds that followed, Pete believed he would die. People don't survive automobile accidents at 70 miles an hour, so how could anyone survive a plane whirling out of control at 150 miles per hour?

It was all a blur to him. He could now hear the screams of his fellow passengers as the screeching metal and sound of impact began to lessen.

The horrifying sounds continued to ring in his ears as the plane continued to fall apart each foot it slid forward on the runway.

Finally Pete sensed the plane slowing. Was it too early to celebrate the fact that he'd survived the crash? Any thoughts of him being the only survivor were quickly erased when the cries and screams from behind him continued to ring out.

The plane rolled one violent, final time, leaving Pete to

ponder the irony—just when he thought he'd survived the crash, he would probably be crushed underneath a pile of twisted metal. Pete found himself upside down as the plane skidded across the runway the last few feet before it stopped. He heard a loud thump and felt the impact of something graze the top of his head.

It sounded like two cars colliding at 15 miles per hour. It wasn't a loud pop, but the distinct sound of bending metal was unforgettable.

Pete tucked his head, fearing the ceiling (or floor) was collapsing over his head. As he tried to shield his head, he felt a warm trickle coming from his forehead. He thought it was sweat until a stream began running down his face and reached into the corner of his mouth.

The plane finally come to a rest. Pete instinctively reached up to feel where the blood was coming from. He could feel a soft gooey part of his scalp where hair was supposed to be.

He reached for his seat belt and unlocked it and dropped to the ground. With a feeling of terror and guilt, Pete now turned his attention, for the first time since impact, to Danny. The crash was so violent, he'd locked himself in his own personal crisis.

He saw Danny hanging upside down. The cabin was dark, but he could see light coming in from the upper right corner of the plane where a section had bent and twisted a five-foot gap in the side of the plane.

Pete reached up and released Danny from his seat belt. His lifeless body dropped into Pete's arms.

He made his way toward the light. He found the exit and walked with Danny in his arms a good 50 yards away from the plane.

The sun had just set on Salt Lake Valley. But it was still light enough to see his breath.

Pete could see emergency vehicles screaming down the runway toward the plane.

Without giving it a second thought, Pete took off his

jacket and laid it on the ground, shielding Danny from the cold grass. Just before he laid him down, he heard Danny let out a small moan.

Pete looked up to heaven and said, “Thank you.”

But as he laid him down, his hand slid over the back of Danny’s head.

What he felt shocked him. The back of his head felt as soft as a bean bag. His head absorbed Pete’s touch like a sponge.

“No. Noooo,” Pete cried to himself.

He held Danny’s hand and could hear him moan. His eyes flickered and finally opened.

He looked as though he was trying to focus on Pete, but he kept squinting like he couldn’t focus.

“Daddy,” Danny asked as if he wasn’t sure.

Pete cleared his throat while a lump the size of a softball went down.

“No, it’s me, Pete. Our plane had kind of a rough landing. But it’s ok, we’re on the ground now and we’ll be getting you into a warm bed. I’ll make sure your dad and your mom come. I’ll take care of everything,” he said clearing Danny’s bangs off his forehead.

Danny gave a smile his best effort. He tried to turn his head and look around, but a wincing look of pain stopped him from moving his head any further.

He reached down, felt his fanny pack, and tried to unzip it without looking, without moving his head.

“What do you need?” Pete asked.

“There is a letter to Santa and my present. Can you mail this letter for me?” Danny asked.

“Sure. Yes. Do you want me to open your present from your dad?”

“No, Dad said I can’t.”

“I don’t think he’d mind,” Pete said in an assuring tone.

“What I’d like is for you to give it to my friend Cam. Santa didn’t go to his house last year.”

Pete shook his head in disbelief. Sampson’s had always

done something for the needy at Christmas. There was Sub for Santa, Toys for Tots, the Salvation Army and a variety of other programs. How could that happen? Sampson's always participated in Christmas programs. Pete would have to admit they only did the minimal and only for PR purposes when there was the possibility of financial benefit. But still...

Not that he was naive, but he was surprised to hear a child actually didn't get anything for Christmas with so many programs around.

Pete assured Danny his Santa would visit Cam's house this year.

Then Danny said, "I... have to, to, to tell you somethin'."

Pete lay down beside Danny and lightly hugged him. He tried to keep his own blood from getting on Danny's face.

The gash in Pete's head had subsided a bit, but there was still a small trickle of blood that streaked down his ear and onto his neck.

"Can you. Will you..."

The sound of screams and emergency vehicles arriving made Danny's crackling voice hard to hear.

"What was that?" Pete asked gently a few times. Pete nodded indicating he understood what Danny said.

Then Pete leaned over to respond to Danny, hoping to say something that would take his mind off the crisis, but he was gone.

Chapter 9

Pete shook Danny lightly in hopes he had just passed out. He put his head on Danny's small chest and tried to feel for a heartbeat.

A better idea was to check his pulse. He grabbed his wrist. Nothing. He couldn't detect any breathing. Little Danny's life was over.

Pete stared up at the sky and groaned. "Nooooooo!"

A few short sobs followed which for Pete was an emotional breakdown.

Pete looked over at the plane. Smoke was coming from the main section of the plane. Flames were beginning to flare up around the windows.

A group of 30 to 40 survivors huddled together about 50 yards west of the burning plane. Medical attention was just arriving. There he saw an elderly man who must have been in his early seventies, trying to wave off some medical attention. He was on his feet; apparently he came out of the accident with only a few scratches.

There is no justice, Pete thought. Danny was only seven. He looked down at the boy. His cheeks were still rosy from the cold, his fanny pack still slightly unzipped. To look at him in the position he was in you couldn't tell anything was wrong. Had he not been lying down off an airport runway in Utah in early December, you would think he was sleeping.

"He had his whole life in front of him. Children

shouldn't have to die," Pete sobbed in a low but emotional tone.

He buried his face in his hands.

"Sir, sir...are you okay?"

Most of the medical attention went to the main group of survivors, but a paramedic spotted Pete and Danny.

Terror showed on the young paramedic's face when he looked down at Danny, not sure who to pay attention to first.

Judging by looks alone, Pete figured he could be no more than twenty, even though Pete knew he had to be at least in his late twenties.

By Pete's reaction and the lifeless look of the boy, the paramedic figured he'd check out the boy first and then turn his attention to Pete.

"Hey, I'm Shaun. Where are you hurt?" he asked as he knelt over the boy and checked for a pulse.

He raised his arms and whistled loudly, calling for some help.

"I'm fine," Pete mumbled in a monotone voice.

Wait a second Pete thought. Danny could be revived. Why not? With medical technology changing seemingly every week, there was still hope. There had to be.

Pete offered some information. "It's his head. The back of..."

He stopped in mid-sentence. There would be no miracles today. While Captain Valgardson and his crew did a miraculous job landing Flight 1392, this would be one of 136 casualties.

Shaun didn't say anything. He just tightened his lip and shook his head slightly, indicating it was too late.

The paramedic slumped over with his head down toward his chest. Pete could see he was struggling. Sometimes even those used to working around death have emotions rise to the surface that have long since been buried.

It was unprofessional to get emotional in an emergency scene. How would the victims feel if they saw the paramedic losing it?

Shaun regained his composure and turned his attention to Pete.

"Let me take a look at you. "

There was a four-inch gash on the right side of Pete's scalp. Shaun could see a small fragment of metal still inside the cut. Blood was still oozing out of the wound like lava running down the side of a mountain.

Most of the blood Pete had lost could be seen on the side of his shirt and his arm.

Pete grimaced when Shaun poked around, assessing the damage.

"Do you feel dizzy? Do you remember the circumstances of the flight? Do you have any pain anywhere else besides your head?"

Pete just shook his head. Right now he couldn't care less about himself. When Shaun continued to ask questions, Pete finally said, "I'm fine. There must be someone else who needs your help."

A Red Cross truck pulled up. A man and a woman jumped out of the truck. The woman went right to Danny's body. Shaun shook his head when she looked over for the boy's status.

She picked up the little boy in her arms like a mother carrying a sleeping boy to his bed. She stepped up into the back of the truck and laid him on a makeshift bed dressed with white sheets.

She paused for a moment, marveling at the innocence of Danny. 'He must have been something special' she thought before lifting the sheet over his face and carefully tucking his right arm under the sheet.

Inside the truck, the noise of the commotion surrounding the wreckage was silenced. If you listened quietly you could hear...drip, drip, drip—the sound of tears hitting the white sheet.

Pete climbed in the back of the Red Cross truck as it pulled off to rendezvous with another vehicle. Pete was transferred to another truck with several other passengers who had non life-threatening injuries. The truck sped off to the University of Utah Hospital. The truck Danny was in would make another stop. Unfortunately, Danny had plenty of company—casualties who wouldn't live to tell about the accident.

The bodies were taken to a make-shift morgue at the airport to be identified and claimed by their families.

Shaun hustled back down to a section of the fuselage.

There was a group of National Guardsmen surrounding the plane and searching the wreckage for bodies. Shaun couldn't help but notice there was a small group of five men who looked like they had found a treasure chest buried in the wreckage. They frantically threw off scraps of wreckage. Apparently with the belief someone was under the twisted metal—alive.

Shaun stayed away from the front line. There were already too many people crowding around the opening of the plane where the flames were doing their best to keep rescue workers from inspecting what was left of the wreckage in hopes of finding survivors.

He surveyed the wreckage that was scattered across two runways. Most of the plane ended up just off a runway and into a dirt field that boarded one of the runways. Emergency personnel combed sections of the plane hoping to find someone who had been missed.

The tail section of the plane had broken away from the fuselage. Shaun figured he'd join a group of National Guardsmen that were concentrating on the tail section.

As he approached the section of the plane, he thought he saw a body, still strapped in a seat, engulfed in flames, but he couldn't be sure. The heat kept him a good 20 feet away.

He stepped closer and realized what he saw was a body.

Shaun still had on his surgical gloves, not much good for searching through twisted metal, but he chipped in anyway. There were several bodies being removed from the wreckage. Shaun joined another man who was wearing the camouflage of the National Guard and pushed over a large metal section that was laying on top of a clump of debris.

Shaun flinched like they'd just turned over a rock in the desert and found a nugget of shining gold.

He could see part of a leg that was still only half visible. They both looked at each other with renewed hope and keen fear about what they may find.

They continued to dig for a few seconds, throwing off smaller chunks of metal, until Shaun suddenly stopped.

He could see where the leg ended. It wasn't attached to anything.

As a paramedic, Shaun had been on the scene of several automobile accidents, many too haunting to relive. But this was different. There was so much death. So many people had just lost their lives and being one of the first people to be on the scene stirred a pot of emotions he'd never been conscious of before.

There was nothing more he could do here. He walked back toward the survivors. Many had already been transported to the hospital, but there were still a few dozen that were huddled together. He would try and help them, or at the very least, comfort them.

At this point it's all he could do.

Chapter 10

Pete stared out the window of the University of Utah Hospital, located on the foothills of the Wasatch Mountain Range that borders Salt Lake City on the east.

He had a room with a view. The lights of the city flickered through his window. He thought about Danny. Then he reached down to the side of his bed and pulled out the letter that Danny gave him to mail.

Dear Santa: This is Danny again. I thought I would write ta you again. Just ta see if you got my last letter. Last year my friend Cam didn't get nothin' for Christmas. Says you were probly to bisy to come to his house.

I hope you have time to go to his house this year. You can go to his house befor mine. Last year you came to my house but I guess you couldn't find his house.

Thanks again for the legos. I still play with them evry day.

P.S. I'll leave some cookies out for you again. Is chocklit chips ok, or do you want somethin else?

Thanks a lot Santa.

See you soon.

Love Danny.

Pete finished reading the letter but continued to stare at the words as though there were was some secret code he was trying to decipher.

Finally, he folded up the letter and clutched it in his right hand.

He peered out the window again and thought about Christmas and Danny's simple wish. He just wanted Santa to visit his friend. He had been brought to a realization of a thought that never occurred to him before—how many children go without each Christmas? How many children go to the stores and see the Christmas decorations all over town, watch "Santa Claus is Coming to Town" on TV along with the other specials and are then forgotten, almost tortured with the hype? What they must go through to know that Santa doesn't care about them. What an empty feeling it must be.

Even though Pete was single and had no children of his own, and usually spent the holidays with his aging mother, he always viewed the Christmas season as the highlight of the year. Christmas wasn't just for kids, but it was never meant to be celebrated without kids.

Pete wasn't much different from other people who thought Christmas organizations and church groups filled the needs of children during the holiday season.

By meeting Danny, he realized he was wrong. In a lonely hospital room far from home, Pete came to the realization of many things. He wanted to make a difference with his life and not just on Sampson's bottom line.

He felt like he'd been missing something. Now he'd found out what it was. His head was bandaged and stitched up, but other than a few scrapes, he was in pretty good shape.

It was remarkable, really, how things happened—switching seats with Danny. As far as he could tell, he was the only one in his section that survived the accident.

He had been wrestling with his guilt—somehow protesting that he cheated death, while Danny and many others all around him never had a chance to live.

Was there a reason why he survived? Perhaps there was

something God wanted him to do that no one else could do?

That was the only thing that made sense. He reflected on that thought for five minutes, ten, then twenty-five. An hour. Why was he spared?

What could he possibly do with the rest of his life to justify this miracle?

Word spread fast, as fast as a California brush fire. Flight 1392 went down. The advanced warning had given the news media ample time to set up a variety of cameras and feeds to CNN, ABC, NBC, CBS, Fox and other outlets.

Ben called Rick into his office. "What flight was Danny on?"

"I don't know. Why?"

"What airline was he flying?" Ben asked.

"I think it was American."

"I hope so. I just heard on the radio a plane went down. It was something like American Sky West, or Western Sky Air."

"Western Sky Air," Rick thought. That sounds familiar. "Please God, no," Rick thought to himself. "Don't let it be Western Sky Air."

Rick began to feel lightheaded like he'd just stood up too fast. He also felt queasy and claustrophobic. "Air. I need air," he thought to himself.

He darted for the exit and walked out the door of the office into a cold breeze, but he didn't notice the temperature.

Think. How could I find out what airline Danny was on?

The more Rick tried to think how he could find out, the less progress he made. Finally, logic took over. He'd call Tina. She would know.

He went back into the office and found Ben watching CNN. It was live coverage of the disaster.

The words, "Western Sky Air Flight 1392," were left up on the screen like the time and score of a football game.

The camera focused on a reporter doing a live shot with

a perfect background—emergency lights.

Rick couldn't wait any longer. "I've got to use your phone. How do I dial out?"

"Dial nine then the number. When you get the tone, dial 4175."

Ben walked closer to the TV and turned down the sound so he could barely hear the TV while Rick made the call.

"A group of survivors have been taken to the hospital. The response has been tremendous. The National Guard, Red Cross, emergency crews, fire departments and paramedics from several surrounding towns have joined in. There's no shortage of help, but it still wasn't enough to save some from the fiery wreckage of Flight 1392."

The lady continued in an excited tone. "The airlines haven't released an official number of survivors. All I can tell you is there have been about 70-85 passengers transported to nearby hospitals."

"What was that number again when you hear the tone?" Rick asked.

"4175."

Rick looked over at the TV and saw the replay of the crash—the plane hitting the asphalt and rolling down the runway; a ball of fire bursting from the rear of the plane. The footage was unbelievable.

He was now quite sure Danny left on Western Sky Air, but he had no idea of the flight number.

"Hi, you've reached 272-4453, please leave a message at the beep."

"Tina, it's Rick. Call me. I need to talk to you. It's an emergency. I'll either be at (702) 366-2451, or 364-3409. Please call me right away."

Ben wrote down the number that flashed on the screen for "family members only" concerning flight information of 1392.

"Rick, I've got the number. You can call and see if that was Danny's flight."

Rick trembled as he held the piece of paper in his hands.

His stomach rumbled like it was protesting a bad meal. He felt as nervous as he was the time he called Cindy Felt and asked her out on his first date. He was so nervous, he stumbled over his words and stuttered. Cindy sensed it was hard on him and quickly agreed, taking the pressure off the situation.

But this was different. A "no" from Cindy would have been hard to get over. A "yes" (Danny was a passenger on 1392) would be something he couldn't live with.

His palms were wet with sweat. His fingers shook as he tried to punch in the numbers—1-800-455-9000. He closed his eyes when he heard the phone ring. Ben could see Rick's lips moving ever so slightly.

He bowed his head and joined his brother in a silent prayer. Ben had always looked out for his little brother. But he knew if he lost Danny, he might lose Rick and just when it looked like he was finally making something of his life.

"You have called Western Sky Air. If you are calling about flight information of Flight 1392, please stay on the line and a representative will be right with you.

"To better serve the needs of family members, we ask that only family members of passengers of Flight 1392 stay on the line. Others requesting flight information from 1392 can call 1-800-345-4423."

Rick nearly hung up and called the other number. He wasn't sure Danny was on board, but on second thought, he had a right to know if his son was alive.

"Thank you for holding, this is Dianne. Do you have a family member on board Flight 1392 from LA to Chicago?"

"I think so," Rick said, his voice shaking. "Can you check to confirm he was a passenger?"

"Yes sir. Can you give me his full name please?"

"Yes, Danny Lee McMurtrey."

"One moment sir."

Rick closed his eyes and grimaced in anticipation of pain. It was like he was a little boy and had just been taken over his father's knee—waiting for that first stinging blow.

"Sir," Dianne said.
"Yes, I'm here."

Chapter 11

When Tina arrived at O'Hare, she looked around for a monitor with flight information. Knowing her luck, Danny's flight had been delayed, or worse, canceled.

But that's why Tina insisted on getting Danny a non-stop flight. She wasn't taking any chances of him getting lost in an airport during a layover.

Finally, she found Western Sky Air arriving flight information. She scanned the screen, but couldn't find any.

Somehow she'd missed it. She looked again.

Flight 1392, LA to Chicago was blinking. "Please see a Western Sky Air representative."

"What did that mean?" Tina wondered as she looked around for a Western Sky Air representative.

She spotted a Western Sky Air counter and began walking toward it when she heard what sounded like a lady crying faintly.

Tina picked up her brisk pace. She was now walking as fast as she could but only for a few steps before she broke into a dead run, as she approached the Western Sky Air counter.

To avoid a scene, Western Sky Air representatives were sternly instructed not to give out any information on Flight 1392.

Instead, the airlines had set up a room where family members would get the news.

A representative escorted Tina to the room. There must

have been 25 Western Sky Air reps. Most were wearing red vests, the airline's colors. Some had white shirts and red ties and some were wearing business suits.

The airline employees outnumbered family members in the room two to one.

Tina had arrived 30 minutes before 1392 was supposed to land. Soon the room would fill up. Tina looked around at the group of strangers.

The mood was like that of a funeral. One of the men wearing a suit, who looked like an airline employee, was nervously tapping his feet. He occasionally looked up to see who had come into the room. His eyes were red—red enough to see through his glasses.

A young woman held a toddler in her arms and rocked it gently trying to keep it from crying. Tina went to the corner of the room so she could be alone.

She was surprised to see a teenage boy, who looked to be 17, playing with his keys, twirling them around his thumb. The hair on the top of his head was dyed blonde, while the rest of his head was shaved. He wore oversized pants and a dress shirt what wasn't tucked in.

Tina looked around the room like she was lost, like she didn't belong. She'd managed to maintain her composure until she saw a priest. Then she cried out loud openly.

An older man with patches of white hair on the sides and thick brown glasses gently asked Tina if she needed some information on Flight 1392?

"What's going on? Did it crash?"

The man introduced Tina to another, Keith Whitlock, whose unenviable task was to oversee the notification of family members about the status of passengers on Flight 1392.

Keith was in his late forties. He only had a touch of gray on the sides of his neatly trimmed hair. He wore gold wire-rimed glasses and had a gentle demeanor. Whoever put him in charge of breaking the good or horrible news to the loved ones, would be in line for a casting job in Hollywood. He was a perfect fit. He was part minister, part gentle father, part good Samaritan.

As father of four and grandfather of three, he was sparked to an even greater sense of compassion to the mothers, fathers, brothers, sisters, boyfriends, fiancees and friends that were being funneled into his hands.

He gently put his arm around Tina and led her back to a section of the room that was separated into cubicals. He was joined by a woman, who had been brought in by the airlines to help counsel and offer emotional support.

Tina tried to keep from crying out loud, but it was no use. When you have a son in the army and someone in uniform shows up at your door, it means only one thing.

The only factor that kept Tina from completely losing it was the uncertainty. Maybe he missed the flight. Knowing Rick, he probably didn't get Danny to the airport on time.

"Please sit down," the man said.

"There was a problem with Flight 1392."

Tina cut in and let out a few short sobs.

"The plane had to make an emergency landing in Salt Lake City," the man continued. "It's not entirely clear what went wrong but the pilot was able to land the plane; however, it was a little rough."

"There were many survivors. We're still trying to get a list of those on board."

Tina stared at the floor in disbelief. The words, "There were many survivors" echoed in her head. "Many, many..."

If there were many survivors, that meant there were fatalities. How bad was this accident? At least there was hope.

"I believe my son was on board. He's only seven. His name is Danny McMurtrey. Danny Lee McMurtrey.

The man had a clipboard. He thumbed through some pink pages. Suddenly his finger stopped on a name.

Tina's countenance sunk.

"We do show him as a passenger ma'am."

"Is he okay? I want to talk to him. I want to go to Salt

Lake right now. Do you have any flights?"

"We're arranging for a flight right now and you can be assured that we're doing our best to take care of your boy."

"How many survivors are there?"

"We're still getting the reports in now. You can be assured as soon as we know, you will know. We have hundreds of qualified people on the scene who know what they're doing. They're working as fast and accurately as they can."

Tina nodded.

"When can I leave? I want to fly to Salt Lake immediately."

"If you will have a seat over there (the man pointed to a section of chairs where nearly a dozen people were waiting), we'll let you know when you can leave."

Shaun's work at the wreckage sight was done. The area had been inundated with National Guard, paramedics, fireman and Search and Rescue teams. All that was left to do was clear the debris of the wreckage, and the most cumbersome task of all—ID the dead.

The adrenaline from working on the crash sight was wearing off. Now comes the tough part, dealing with the afterthoughts.

These are memories that carve a place in a person's mind, leaving tattoo-like scars that may not be visible on the skin, but never really go away.

Shaun found a place to sit—on the floor inside a baggage area that had been turned into a makeshift morgue.

"So many people died today," he thought to himself. Then he wondered about their families. They don't even know yet. They're probably going about their lives without even a clue of what had just happened.

How their world will be different.

Then he thought of Danny and his parents. "Can you imagine making that phone call," he thought.

"You okay?" a soft, young voice of a woman called out.

Shaun was deep in thought, with his head buried in his hands. He looked up for a split second and nodded at the woman, not paying much attention to her piercing smile and blonde hair. She was wearing a white dress, much like that of a nurse's outfit.

"Thank you. You'll never know how much you helped out today," she said.

Shaun nodded again, then returned to his self consolation. Finally, he regained his composure and lifted his head up and saw four firemen standing in a circle talking to a man in a three-piece suit. He saw a man and a woman each holding a clipboard walking up and down the aisle of bodies covered with sheets.

He heard the door open and saw the woman in white holding the hand of a young boy, leading him out the door. The boy tapped the woman on her arm, showing off a giant bubble he'd blown with his gum.

The woman poked the bubble with her finger. Both of them giggled as they walked out the door. The light coming in from outside was so bright, like coming out of the darkness of a movie theater into the noon-day sun.

The door closed behind them.

Shaun got up and got his coat. There was nothing left for him to do.

He walked toward the door, turned the handle and stepped into the darkness. He felt like a failure. He'd only helped one person (Pete) and anyone could have done that. It was just a few cuts and a mild concussion. Nothing even a first-year med student couldn't have done.

Then there was the boy. He reflected back on the scene. Could he have done anything to save him? What would he do differently? Did he give up too soon?

He felt guilty, more than he ever had in all his eight years on the job. If he had handled the situation better, made a quicker assessment, he could have been a hero to someone. He could have made a difference. Then maybe he would feel better about himself now.

As Shaun began to walk toward his car like a lost sightseer, he thought about the nurse. She was wearing white. None of the other paramedics, Red Cross workers, or airport personnel were wearing all white.

At the time, he didn't think twice about the bright light. But it was dark. There were no lights on outside the door.

He looked toward the north and saw a large group of temporary lights set up on the runway as the cleanup process was still in high gear, but the lights made only a distant glow.

The crews would work around the clock until the airport opened again and as much data about Flight 1392 could be obtained.

Then the words, "Thank you," rang in his mind. It was as clear as if he were talking to someone. "Thank you," the young women's voice called out again.

A warm feeling came over Shaun, like the sun rising over the Wasatch mountains, bringing warmth to the desert valley.

Shaun scanned the airport as if he were looking for someone. He stopped walking as if he finally understood what had just happened and for the first time smiled.

Chapter 12

Keith Whitlock picked up the phone and nodded. He looked down at his clipboard. He lifted up a page and used his finger to find the name "Danny Lee McMurtrey."

He got out a red marker and drew a line under his name.

He sighed. "This may be the hardest one," he thought to himself.

There were a variety of clergy on hand who had graciously offered their services. There was one man who was talking with an airline representative. He went over and whispered something into the man's ear. His facial expression immediately changed to one of disappointment. He then nodded his head.

Keith saw Dianne Hoover, a psychologist, who'd written several books on grief, including one on rebuilding life after the death of a child.

She was perfect for the situation. He explained the circumstances to her. He waved his head toward Tina, who was sitting quietly by herself on a chair staring at the ground.

Dianne nodded.

Keith knelt next to her and gently called out her name while he put his hand on her shoulder.

She looked up, eyes red and a Kleenex held up to her nose.

"Can I talk to you for a minute?"

She didn't say a word, but got up and followed Keith. There was a small office that Dianne and the minister were already in.

Keith's pulse pounded. He hadn't run five miles in 20 years, but his heart was racing like he'd just tried to run five miles up a mountain hillside.

He opened the door and made introductions. Tina sensed what was about to happen and began crying out loud.

Dianne grabbed her hand. "Tina. It's okay." She could do no more than wait, like a mother holding a child, waiting for the sting of a scraped knee to subside.

When Tina regained her composure, Keith spoke.

"Our crews in Salt Lake City have been working as fast as possible double checking the list of passengers on board, making sure there have been no mistakes."

Suddenly Tina was filled with hope. Maybe he wasn't on board. Thank you for screwing up Rick. She would give Rick a kiss for making Danny miss his flight. And when she saw Danny again, there wouldn't be enough time in a day to hug him. She would never let a day go by where she wouldn't get on her knees and thank God for his presence.

"We have confirmed that your son Danny McMurtrey was a passenger on Flight 1392," Keith paused unintentionally, his voice shaking, "I'm sorry, we believe he passed away during the accident. We'll need you to identify the body."

Tina slipped out of Dianne's grasp and fell to her knees.

She looked up at the ceiling, tears rushing down her cheeks like the gutters on a street after a summer thunderstorm, but not a sound came out. It was like she was struggling for breath, as if someone had just knocked the wind out of her.

Chapter 13

The two days in the hospital had left Pete feeling like his hospital room was on Jupiter. It may as well have been. The emptiness and isolation from people he knew was suffocating.

Two days of being awakened every time he'd finally managed to get to sleep. Two days of getting poked, pestered and tested all while eating hospital food, had left Pete plenty of time for soul searching.

He'd come to one shocking discovery. He'd lived 42 years and how much of an impact had he had on others? He failed at his marriage. He had no children. The phone to his hospital room rang just twice since he'd been there–once from his mother and once from his secretary, who wanted to know what to do about his schedule for the rest of December, and if he was doing okay.

Pete struggled to shake off the gloom that surrounded his hospital room. With the view from his room, he could see neighborhoods that were decorated with Christmas lights. He looked down over the city where the lights melted together. There was one bright glow that stood out like a spotlight in a row of flashlights. It was historic Temple Square, always a spectacular sight at night, but made even more so with hundreds of thousands of extra Christmas lights covering the grounds around Salt Lake City's most famous sight.

Pete had been to Temple Square once and passed by it

several times, but tonight it took on a different look.

He couldn't seem to take his eyes off the lights. He was mesmerized. His eyes focused on the lights as if he were watching a movie.

Two days had passed and finally feelings of failure and emptiness were replaced with ones of excitement and hope.

Pete had an idea. He would dedicate a section of a store that's sole purpose was to give back to the community. A full-time Santa could be there to visit the kids.

They could rewrap many of the presents that were returned and tossed in a damaged basket and discounted 30 percent. It would be better to write those off and give them away.

It would be great PR and could actually increase business.

"Support the store that supports your community." Slogans began to pop into Pete's mind. There had to be a way to make a profit on this.

The instincts that made Pete a great businessman tried to put a spin on it.

We could have a donation bucket that would be used to pay for the Santa and the giveaways. It wouldn't cost the store a dime.

It didn't take Pete long to reject that idea. He thought of Danny and of his little friend Cam.

As CEO of a major department store, he now felt an obligation to use his position to create something positive. To use his skills to help others. That could be his new "Golden Touch." Pete pushed the button and buzzed the nurse. He needed a pencil and a piece of paper. He had to write down his ideas, and fast. He didn't want to forget a single one.

This was something they could do all year long, not just for Christmas. He planned on keeping it open year-round.

They would have a giant candy jar. Every kid would get to grab a piece and during the holidays, there would be a present for everyone.

There were still so many things to work out. How would

they discern between the needy children and the greedy children? He'd figure something out. What about the costs?

The hours passed by—2:00 a.m., 3:00 a.m., 4:00 a.m., 4:30. He had three pages of notes. By the time he fell asleep he had a plan.

As Rick stared out over the ocean, every song he heard on the radio pricked his heart. There was now such an enormous hole in his heart where he just had the life squeezed out of him.

The last hour and a half Rick sat in his car with the radio turned up as loud as the speakers in his 1981 Chevy Citation would allow.

He finally got out of his car and walked down the moonlit sand toward the high tide.

He took off his shoes, carelessly discarded them on the sand, and headed toward the hissing sound as the waves broke and rolled up on the sand.

Rick waded into the waves with no thought of the chilly water. He was hoping the cold water would take away some of the pain he felt in his heart.

He waded out to his knees and contemplated whether he should just keep walking—right out into the ocean and disappear. After all, the reason for living was now gone. He couldn't think of a single reason why he shouldn't just keep going, right out into the ocean and never look back.

A full moon shone bright on a clear cool night. The temperature dropped to 50 degrees and a slight breeze was blowing in the waves at high tide.

Tears poured down his face. A few sobs escaped as he finally cried out loud. Why, God? Danny was so little. So precious, so full of love, of life.

He looked up at the moon and opened his mouth as if to speak. His lips moved but no sound came out.

His head sunk toward the water as all the emotion of Danny's death poured out like a two-liter bottle of soda that had been shaken up.

"Oh, God, he had so much to live for. Why couldn't it have been me? I wish to God it was me. I've had my turn. I've had my chances. Why couldn't I have been with him? He was all alone."

In the early morning hours on the beach, Rick came to a conclusion. He was a failure. He couldn't think of a single thing he'd done that turned out right.

He was a lousy student in high school. He didn't want to go to college. He couldn't keep a job. His restlessness wouldn't let him stay focused on one thing very long.

He was 26-years old and broke. He never had a job long enough to pay child support. He didn't have any talents. He was a marginal athlete. Heck, he was cut from his high school football team in his senior year of all things. He failed at his marriage too.

Maybe Tina was right. In one of their final confrontations, she labeled him a "loser."

He could hear her voice, "always have been, always will be."

She was right. He should have been working three jobs to provide his son with a better life. He should have been able to do so much more. A wave of guilt now overwhelmed him at the thought. He should have done much more with Danny.

Now it's too late. There will be no second chances. The finality of his poor choices now reached up and slapped him across the face.

Rick began thinking back to the time Danny was born. He remembered how angry he was when Tina said she was pregnant. He also remembered his first shameful thought. What about an abortion? He wasn't ready for a kid.

He was so ashamed now to think of how selfish he was. "Shows how much I know," he thought to himself.

What he thought would only complicate his life and make him miserable, turned out to be the greatest thing that had ever happened to him.

He remembered the first time Danny laughed. They were at McDonald's and had sat close to the play area. Little

Danny was in his car seat/carrier watching kids go down a slide when he smiled and let go the cutest little laugh.

Tina and Rick looked at each other and then broke out in laughter in unison. That was nearly seven years ago, yet it now seemed like seven days ago.

There was the time when he tried to take him to a Chicago Cubs game. The Cubs' rival, the St. Louis Cardinals, were in town and all the bleacher seats were long gone by the time he tried to buy two cheap tickets.

The only seats left were standing room only. There were tickets to be had from scalpers walking the street, but instead of standing behind some pole with an obstructed view, the two spent the next two hours playing catch (they both had brought their gloves with the anticipation of catching a home run ball) out on Waveland Avenue.

Two baseballs left the park that day. One actually landed only 20 yards away from Danny. He heard the roar of the crowd and looked up holding his glove in the air, while he tried to shield his eyes from the sun with his other hand.

He never saw the ball hit the street, but he did see it roll under a parked car. He started over toward the ball, but was quickly passed and knocked down on the street by a mob of kids, who were regulars on Waveland Ave.

Danny scraped his elbow and the palm of his right hand. He got up and once he saw the blood on his palm, he broke into tears.

Rick sat down on the curb and worked on getting some of the tiny rocks out of his hand that broke through the skin.

One lucky boy, who looked to be about 12, crawled under the car and held up his trophy high in the air for everyone to see. He looked around for a TV camera. Kids scrambling for homerun balls always made for a good TV shot.

As he passed by Danny and saw Rick working on his hand and trying to quiet his tears, the boy made a decision his friends would later call "crazy."

He walked up to Danny, kneeled down so he could look

him in the eyes. "I'm not sure if I knocked you down or not, but here, I want you to have this ball. I'm sorry."

Danny's eyes lit up and his tears instantly stopped like someone had just turned off the faucet.

Rick smiled and tugged on the Cubs hat that rested on the boy's head. "Thanks. That's very big of you."

The boy could already hear the other kids talking. "He just gave the ball to that kid. What a dummy. What is he thinking?"

He would hear about it for weeks to come, but nothing anyone could say replaced the feeling of how he felt when he gave Danny the ball.

All the memories gushed out now. One led to another then to another and another and another.

It was now 6:00 a.m. The moon and stars had given way. Rick could see the sun was trying to rise. Soon the warm beams of the sun would shine down on the ocean. Rick never remembered the morning being so clear. He never remembered feeling so alone.

He looked out as far as he could see in the ocean, tears streaking down his face, his lip trembling.

"Oh, God...He was my only son.... He was my life...Can you possibly know how I feel?"

Chapter 14

Rick picked up his shoes and walked toward the beach one final time. He looked out into the ocean wishing he could feel the strength of the waves as they crashed on the shore.

His sweat pants were now completely dry, but he was still cold, feeling the effects of a brisk night at the beach with no jacket, just a sweatshirt to keep him warm.

His grief had finally given way to his emotionally-drained body. All he wanted right now was to sleep. He reasoned to himself that he couldn't hurt like this if he was asleep.

Sleep would be his painkiller.

As Rick turned his back to the ocean, he felt the chill of the ocean water run past his feet and finally run out of energy about 10 feet in front of him.

The wave broke forward 15 feet further up the sand than any of the other waves.

The shock of the cold water only lasted for a brief second, then was gone along with the retreating water.

But just as the surprise of the water left his feet, he felt a sharp pain in his right foot.

"Ouch."

Rick's first thought was that he'd stepped on a piece of glass. It wasn't the first time. But as he bent over he saw what he had stepped on—a small three-inch seashell.

It had a swirl of pink to it but it was mostly peach

colored with a touch of white mixed in.

It was perfect. No chips, no cracks or pieces missing. Seashells wash up every morning on the shore, but not like this one. Not in California. He continued to brush the sand off of it as he walked to his car.

The shell had seven spikes on the outside and curved around into the center as if a sculptor had created it.

Seven. Rick put his finger on a small spike and counted. One, two, three, four, five, six, seven.

Seven.

He held it up in the air as if he were checking under a car and as he did he felt the first rays of the morning sunshine hit his back.

The sun shined off the shell and reflected into his eyes. His whole body began to warm up. It was like the sun had brought a new life to him. The darkness was gone.

He felt the warm beams invade his body like he'd just walked out from under the shade of a tree and into the sun.

It circulated through his whole body, finally resting in the iciest part of all—his heart.

Something was happening. He could feel it. He had chills going up and down his arms and he felt a tingling sensation like someone was running a feather up and down his legs.

Then in his mind he heard Danny's voice, and the last words he heard Danny say echoed in his mind. "Love you Dad. Love you Dad. Love you...Love you...Love you Dad."

The words brought renewed power and strength.

"Woo, woo, woo."

He could feel Danny's hand as he gave him the best pal hand shake.

Without hearing the words, Rick had a feeling that Danny was now okay. The shell had become a gift from Danny. Now he would always be near.

"I like your hair like that. Did you get it cut?" Pete asked.

Janice blushed a little. "Yeah, I just got my bangs trimmed."

"So is all your Christmas shopping done?" Pete asked.

"Uh, nooo. I'm usually not done until Christmas Eve. I don't want to break tradition," Janice said.

Pete smiled.

"Do you think you can read my scribbling and type up these notes?" Pete asked in a gentle tone.

Janice, his secretary for the last three years, replied with a surprised grin. "I'm sure I can, maybe not word for word."

"Great," Pete said as he walked into his office.

"Wow, he's in good mood," she thought. "That's strange."

Pete has always been cordial, but rarely friendly. Always professional, but never personal.

There was something different about him. She noticed it right away even before he said a word.

She smiled. Her countenance was uplifted as she began to type.

Pete spent the rest of the morning on the phone. He didn't bother taking a lunch. He was on the phone from 11:30 to 2:30, getting the ground work laid out.

He decided the Sampson's on Michigan Ave. would be the store where his plan would be implemented.

He sent out the following memo to the store manager.

> "Please have ALL managers and as many employees as possible present tomorrow at 9:00 a.m. for a 30-minute briefing. This is of the utmost urgency. Thank you."
>
> Pete Sampson.

He met the next morning with over 70 employees and managers.

"Your store is about to become the most important store in the entire Sampson Department Store chain. I have chosen this store and you people as the ones to carry out a very special program, one that means a great deal to me."

Pete began to choke up.

Suddenly the hourly employees who weren't listening, paid attention when they heard his voice crack.

"As some of you may know I was on Flight 1392. You know, that one that crashed. The one on TV and in all the newspapers."

He now had everyone's undivided attention.

"I was very lucky to have survived the accident, but there were many others who weren't as fortunate."

Pete pulled out his handkerchief in anticipation of losing control of his emotions.

"Flight 1392's destination was Chicago. Your neighbors and our friends have had their lives forever changed with the loss of their loved ones. Now at a time when there should be great celebration and joy, there is tremendous heartbreak and sadness.

"I'm giving your managers the outline of a new program we are implementing in your store that I believe will help those in our community to better celebrate this great holiday season. It's important that each of you catch the spirit of this program, because each of you has the opportunity to change the lives of those who shop here.

"I know some of you are only working here for some extra holiday spending money and this job doesn't mean that much to you, but I'm asking you, I'm pleading for your cooperation. Please, while you're here, help your customers have a positive experience. Not so they'll come back and sales will go up, but because you feel a love for this season. Then when you go home or move onto other job opportunities, you can take with you the spirit you feel this holiday season.

"It's come to my attention that many of those in our community don't have a merry Christmas. Depression runs high on what should be the happiest time of the year. I'd like to do our part to change that.

"In the next few days, you will be briefed on the

program we are implementing. We will be calling on some of you as part of your shift to work in this program. Those of you who are interested in helping the children in our community have a merry Christmas, please see Russell Prestwich. He is the manager I've asked to help me coordinate this program.

"If any of you are willing to volunteer your time to help in this program, I can make you this promise: If you don't think your time was well spent in this project, I want you to come and see me and I will personally pay you time and a half from my own pocket.

"I anticipate the response will be tremendous.

"I hope I can count on your cooperation. I thank you for coming. Please help yourself to the doughnuts and drinks in the back, that is if Russ Prestwich hasn't eaten them all yet."

The employees, who loved to tease Russ about his doughnut habit and his pot belly, all erupted with laughter.

"I'll be in the store all afternoon if you have any questions."

On the back row, one of the employees turned to another and said, "Geeze, what's with him? Does he really think anyone is going to work here without getting paid? Right."

The other employee wiped her eyes and smiled as she looked for a sign-up sheet to volunteer.

Chapter 15

The phone rang once, twice, three, four, five and six times, but Tina just sat on her couch in her sweats, her hair up, looking like it was Saturday morning and a phone call just woke her up.

At first she looked over at the phone as if she actually thought about answering it. But she returned her attention back to the photos of Danny.

Tina smiled when she came to the one taken at the hospital. She was holding Danny for the first time. She laughed out loud when she turned her attention to the picture at the zoo. Danny was hanging out of his stroller pointing at a ball in the pool that a group of seals were playing with.

Her heart then sank as she turned the page and saw a picture of Rick and Danny at a Cubs game. He was only four and it was his first baseball game. He had a little Cubs hat and a tiny little baseball glove.

She thought about Rick. They'd twice talked on the phone since the accident. But both of them were reluctant to express their feelings to each other.

Tina knew he was hurting, but she didn't have the strength to extend him a hand. Too much emotional damage had been done for them to ever share their feelings with each other, even at a time like this.

The answering machine finally picked up.

"Hello, Tina, this is Pete Sampson. I sat next to your boy

on Flight 1392."

She jumped off the couch and for the first time in three days showed signs of life.

"Hello, hello, are you still there?"

"Is this Tina?"

"Yes, it is. What were you saying?"

"I was a passenger on the flight. I sat next to your son."

Tina didn't say a word. She stood there tense, like a prisoner with a blindfold on, waiting to be executed. Her heart was beating so loud, she was sure Pete could hear it on the other end of the receiver.

"There's some things I'd like to tell you. Some things I think you should know. Is there a time when I can come over?"

"Sure. Whenever, any time."

"This is urgent, would it be imposing if I came over this afternoon?"

"No," Tina sniffled. "That's fine. I'll be here all afternoon."

"How about 1:30?"

"Okay, I'll see you then."

"Wait, what's your address?"

Tina gave Pete instructions and quickly began to clean up her apartment. She only had two hours to take a shower, get dressed and look presentable.

Pete stepped up to the door, paused, looked at his watch. It was exactly 1:30.

He pushed the doorbell and could hear what looked like scrambling inside the apartment.

He stood on the doorstep in a black suit with a black and maroon tie. A long tan trench coat helped the Chicago wind bounce off him. He could have passed for an FBI agent had he put on a pair of sunglasses.

Finally, Tina opened the door and smiled.

Pete could see she'd been crying. Her eyes were red and her mascara was slightly smeared.

"Pete?" she sheepishly asked.

"Yes," he said with a reassuring smile.

"Please come in. Here let me take your coat."

Pete sat down and began looking around the room. He counted 10 pictures of Danny that decorated the apartment, before Tina took his attention away from the room and back to her.

"So do you work in Chicago?" Tina asked.

"Yeah, I've got an office downtown."

Tina nodded.

"I work for Sampson's Department Stores."

"Oh great. Yeah, I love Sampson's. I shop there all the time."

Pete doubted that, but appreciated her effort to make him feel comfortable.

"So are you the manager there, or..."

"I'm actually the CEO of the company," Pete said.

He wasn't bragging, he was just setting Tina up for what would come.

"Wow," Tina said, obviously impressed.

"I was coming back from a business trip in the LA area when I got on Flight 1392."

Tina was trying to keep her composure. She was determined not to lose it in front of Pete.

"That's where I met your boy, Danny."

Too late, a tear escaped from Tina's eye as Pete continued.

"I don't have any children of my own. Heck, I've never really liked children. The flight was overbooked and the stewardesses were going to have to pull passengers off the plane."

Pete chuckled a little to himself. "Danny was the last passenger on. I always book two First Class seats, because there's many times when I have an assistant travel with me or I'll need the room to work on projects. Danny took the seat next to me."

Tina now looked relieved. She was beginning to get a glimpse of Danny's final minutes of life, something that was haunting her. As a mother, she agonized over those final minutes of Danny's life when she wondered if he was scared and if he suffered. Did he say anything about her just before he died? Or was he killed instantly?

"What a great kid," Pete said with a beaming smile. "He drew Christmas pictures. One for his friend Cam. One of his dad and one of Christmas here at home with you."

Another laugh slipped out. "You should have seen his Santa. The sack of presents he was trying to stuff down a chimney was actually bigger than the house."

Tina laughed as she cleared her tears with a Kleenex.

"You know what gets me the worst is that I wasn't there for him in those last few minutes. I'm sure he was scared. I can't imagine how he felt," Tina said as she shook her head in sadness.

"Well, I can tell you we were all pretty scared in those last few minutes before we went down," Pete said. "But it all happened so fast. Just know this—he didn't suffer. In the final minutes before we landed..." Pete paused. He wasn't going to tell her, tell anyone about what he'd done. But he needed her to know. His conscience cried out for someone to share its load. The tremendous guilt he felt was like someone was stacking bricks on his chest.

Sometimes it was hard to breath just to think about it.

"I have to tell you something," Pete said.

Tina looked intently on, wondering what had this powerful man so shaken up.

"When it was evident that we were going down, I asked one of the stewardesses which seat, the aisle or the window, was the safest."

Pete paused again, visibly shaken.

A tear escaped and rolled down the side of his cheek. "I've had my chance, you know? I just wanted him to live. He had so much to look forward to. His whole life was ahead of him."

Tina nodded in agreement as he continued.

"The stewardess thought the window seat would be

safer, so I traded Danny places. If only I had just stayed where I was," Pete buried his head in his hands.

"I'm so sorry. I hope you will someday forgive me," Pete cried.

Pete didn't have a handkerchief with him. He had completely lost his composure. This had never happened before. He was in charge of hundreds of stores, he had thousands of employees under him, but here he was now totally at the mercy of his emotions.

Tina moved toward him and embraced him. How could she possibly have anything to forgive him for? It was an incredible act of courage and love. She had never seen anything like it and to think that he was trying to do what he could to save the life of a boy he hardly knew.

She marveled at him. She was in awe of his kindness and his unsung heroic act.

"You actually traded him seats so he had a better chance of living?" Tina asked.

"I'm so sorry," Pete repeated.

Tina pulled away from their embrace and used her hand to clear the tears away from his face.

Tina grabbed Pete's hand and led him to the couch where they thumbed through a photo album. As Tina turned each page, Pete felt like he grew closer to Danny with each picture.

What was it about this boy that was so remarkable? What was this feeling he had about Danny? As he focused on each picture, Danny's life began to take shape as if a jigsaw puzzle was now missing only a few pieces. It was like someone had just pushed an auto focus button on a camera.

Pete had a feeling he couldn't shake. There was something familiar about Danny. The more he thought about it, the more he was sure he knew Danny. He tried to think back.

Somewhere, somehow, he'd seen Danny before. He was sure he'd never met Tina, but he thought back of all the possibilities of where he could have seen him. Maybe at a store, maybe at a Cubs game. Nope. It just didn't seem to fit.

Tina closed the photo album.

What a blessing Pete's presence had been. The healing process was beginning to start.

Tina put her hand on top of Pete's hand and asked, "Will you tell me what happened? How did he die?"

Chapter 16

The room was as dark as a night without the moon and stars. The only light in the room was coming from the red numbers of a clock radio. Soft music could be faintly heard. Pain could be felt.

"Mom, are you going to get up for dinner?" a young voice asked.

"Mom?"

"Mom... Dad and I made dinner. Your favorite—spaghetti and meatballs. It's my favorite too. We thought you'd like it."

Cindy turned over and parted her thick brown hair away from her swollen pink eyes. Her face was pale and her voice was soft.

"I'm sorry. I don't feel much like eating tonight. Thank you for the thought. You're the greatest."

Kyle quietly closed the door and went to report the news to his father.

It looks like it will just be dinner for three again—eleven year-old Kyle, his fifteen-year-old sister Megan, and Dad.

The three family members sat by each other and joined hands in a sign of solidarity. There were two empty chairs.

"Our dear Heavenly Father, we ask thee to bless this food and we are thankful for it. We are thankful for all we have. We acknowledge we are highly blessed among people..."

The father continued. This wasn't a typical blessing on the food given without much thought or feeling.

"We are grateful for the time thou has given us with Susie and ask that thou would take her in thy care and let her know how much we love and miss her. She was so important to our family.

And we ask a special blessing on mom, Kyle and Megan and myself that we may feel of thy spirit and help us to overcome our grief that seems to be so overwhelming at this time."

The father continued. When he finally said, "Amen," there wasn't a dry eye. No one felt like eating, but still all three quietly finished up their plates.

"I remember hearing a popping sound followed by a strong vibration," Pete said. "The plane rattled and shook. At the time there were a few screams, but mostly everyone was quieted with fear."

Tina nodded with interest.

"The captain was frank with us. He told us they'd lost an engine but that the plane was very capable of flying with two engines. I think Danny was scared at first, but the stewardesses were great and after the captain explained the situation," Pete let out a chuckle, "Danny returned to his drawings."

Pete could see a sense of relief on Tina's face.

"It was about 15 minutes later when the captain explained there was some additional damage to the plane and that we would be making an emergency landing in Salt Lake City. I remember Danny looked up at me as if he trusted me. He didn't say a word, but I knew what he was thinking. He wanted to know if we were going to be okay. I nodded my head and assured him we were going to be fine. I said I'd been in situations like this before and it was no problem.

"That was good enough for him. He trusted me completely and once again turned his attention to his drawings. He would stick out his tongue like this," Pete said, doing his best imitation of Danny, which got a half laugh, half cry from Tina.

"He never really knew the danger we were in. In fact, in the last few minutes before we went down," Pete paused while his smile turned into a small laugh, "I remember he had a bubble gum-blowing contest with this girl."

"What?" Tina said curiously.

"This young college girl was sitting just behind the curtain on the first row in coach. She must have seen him and felt like she could help. She gave Danny some gum and challenged him to a bubble gum-blowing contest."

Pete smiled as he recalled what an amazing gesture he thought it was. He now vividly remembered how she deliberately tried to take Danny's mind off what would soon come. He remembered how she comforted the elderly woman that sat next to her in the last few minutes before the crash.

"Who was she? Do you know?"

"No, I wish I did. I don't even know if she survived the crash. All I can remember was she had on a navy blue UCLA sweatshirt and she had long blonde hair with ocean blue eyes. She was like an angel on board."

Tina's mind drifted off as she pictured this girl in her mind. Her concentration was perfect. Her mind clear. She pictured the girl and almost as if she were there, felt her kindness.

As she thought about Pete's comment, "She was like an angel on board," she felt a warm sensation circulate through her body like someone had just ejected her with a shot of sunshine.

Tina had a feeling she had died. Somehow she sensed she was with Danny.

"I guess you didn't know her name or anything," Tina asked.

Pete shook his head. "I didn't remember seeing her with the rest of the survivors, but that doesn't mean much. It was so chaotic that I could have easily missed her. Or she could have been taken to the hospital. I don't know."

Tina was fascinated with this new revelation. She knew she had to know more.

Chapter 17

A construction crew was busy following a blueprint of Pete's plan, measuring, sawing and hammering. Counters had arrived and were being put in place.

A background screen was being set up for photos. Round picnic-type tables were placed in the middle and to the far left were rows of booths. Each booth was set up like a mini carnival.

There were strands of multicolored Christmas lights sitting in a box, ready to line each booth where kids could play games and win prizes. An oven was being installed for making sugar cookies and cupcakes. There were two tables set up for decorating.

A platform was being installed where Santa's throne would soon sit.

A separate crew worked in the middle of the area that had been screened off from the rest of the store. Their focus was on the centerpiece that would complete the project.

The centerpiece had to be just right. Pete would oversee that project himself.

The date to be completed was a little less than a week away on Saturday, December 17.

His office was working on a press release. Pete had been asked by at least a dozen media outlets, both TV and newspapers, for an interview.

He'd said no to all of them, even to one of his better friends, David G. Fletcher at the Chicago Tribune. But he promised if they came to the ribbon cutting of Sampson's new attraction, he would give them all an interview and promised to give them as much time as they needed. He told David he would be first.

Pete knew how to get what he wanted. Now he was using the "Golden Touch" on what he considered the most important project of his life.

Rick walked into Miller and South Jewelers. He hadn't been particular about where he went. Miller and South let him open a line of credit so they got his business.

"You're back," the woman said.

Rick smiled and tried to take a discreet peak behind him to see who she was talking about.

"It turned out great. Wait till you see it."

Rick wondered how the woman remembered him. She wasn't the one who had helped him when he came in before. He remembered seeing her in the store, but was shocked to think she would remember him.

The woman left the counter and went into the back room.

Rick talked to himself. "She remembered me."

He smiled. She was what he thought about when he came to California. Tall, tan and blonde. Well, streaks of blonde ran through her brown hair. It was close enough.

She came back. Rick looked at her name tag "Samantha."

He'd remember that.

Samantha opened the black box.

"It's beautiful. She's going to love it. I must say, it's a perfect Christmas present," Rick took the seashell out of the case and inspected the 14K gold chain that was threaded through a small hole that had been drilled near the top of the shell.

"You're right, it is perfect," Rick said as he touched the shell gently with his thumb and ran his fingers over the seven spikes. "But it's not for my girlfriend, it's for me."

Samantha looked a bit surprised, but could see it had great sentimental value.

"Where did you buy the shell?"

"I didn't, I found it."

"Really?"

"I found it on one of the beaches around here."

"No way. This looks like a West Indian Fighting Conch, but it can't be. "

Rick gave her a puzzled look and waited for a translation. He could see she was fascinated with the shell.

"If I remember right, those are usually found in the Caribbean and in Brazil. You don't find those around here. I would know, I live at the beach."

That was obvious from her tan face accented by her white dress that not only brought out her golden skin, but her green eyes as well.

"I'm a conchologist."

Again Rick gave her a blank stare.

"I collect seashells," Samantha explained. "I probably have over 1,000."

"You're kidding?" Rick said in a shocked tone. "Where on earth do you keep so many?"

"Most of them are in boxes. I love making things out of them. You know a lot of cultures used to use shells as currency. In fact the Romans actually made a purple dye from murex sea snails. They believed cloth colored with this dye was actually more valuable than gold."

Rick nodded with interest and leaned over the counter giving Samantha his undivided attention, even though he didn't have a clue of what she was talking about, but he was impressed she knew so much about seashells. More importantly was that she took an interest in his shell.

She continued to rotate it and marvel at its texture as she talked.

"See," she said, pulling her hair away from her ear and pointing to one of her earrings. It was a skinny two-inch shell, long and narrow. It was a light tan mixed with an off white.

Rick leaned over to take a look. "Wow, that's nice."

"It's called a Powis's Tibia. These are pretty rare in the states, but I thought it would make a perfect earring."

"You're right."

Another couple wandered into the store, cutting their conversation short, but Samantha couldn't resist one last question.

"So tell me, I'm curious, why did you make that into a necklace?"

"It's a present from a very special person. This shell is the most valuable possession I will ever own. Not because there's some rare pearl in it, but because of what it represents."

Samantha listened curiously. Rick stopped, but it was clear she wanted him to continue the story. The couple was still browsing and she was leaning over the counter, hanging on his every word.

"It's from my son. I wanted to make it into a necklace and wear it next to my heart. You see, he's not with me anymore," Rick said. He then paused, trying to decide how much to tell her.

"You may have heard about that plane that crashed. My boy was on that flight. He came out to visit me and was going home to his mother.

"He was blessed with a gift of compassion and kindness. He taught me so many things. You know how they say if you put a seashell to your ear you can hear the ocean? Well, when I listen to this shell with my heart, I believe he will help me find what he had."

Samantha cleared her throat, obviously touched by Rick's story.

"It really is the most beautiful shell I've ever seen. Your boy must have been something special."

Rick nodded, closed the case and handed it back to Samantha to put in a sack.

"Here you go," she said, sharing ownership of the sack with Rick. "If you ever need it cleaned, let me know. I can take care of it for you. "

Samantha let go of the sack and smiled.

Rick began walking to the door past a long display case of diamond rings. Just before he got to the door he looked back and saw Samantha had turned her attention to helping the couple.

She glanced up to see Rick watching her. She talked to the couple but didn't really know what she was saying. All her focus was on Rick. Her conversation with him had moved her. She thought about the seashell, its beauty, its uniqueness. Of all the shells she'd collected, she'd never seen anything quite like it.

She looked up and saw Rick had turned back to wave goodbye.

Rick's heart got his first message.

"Come again," she said.

"I will," Rick said as he waved.

Chapter 18

Pete averaged five hours of sleep for the next five days as he prepared for Dec. 20.

On Sunday, Dec. 19 at 8 p.m., Pete asked Tina to come down to the store.

He greeted her as she pulled up to the front doors.

"Just park you car here. We closed at six," he said as he grabbed her hand and helped her from the car.

She walked into the store. The lights were on in all the sections of the store, except one.

Pete put his hands over Tina's eyes and gave the signal for an employee to turn on the lights.

There it was. Christmas lights blinked and shone across a gateway that read, "Danny's Corner."

Tina put her hands to her mouth in shock. She'd never seen anything like it. It was like a prop for a movie. It was just the way she envisioned Santa's workshop to be like when she was a kid. It was magical. There were so many lights, little white ones wound around artificial pine trees that looked planted on a small snowy slope next to Santa's workshop. There were red, green, orange, blue, and yellow lights. Some blinked furiously, some blinked occasionally and some blinked, it seemed, whenever the lights felt like it.

On the other side across from Santa's workshop was a manger made of old boards from a weathered wooden fence in an effort to give the manger a look of authenticity.

A glow came from one of the windows where Mary and Joseph held baby Jesus. On another slope, three wise men looked up at a bright star hanging from the ceiling of the store that looked like it was 3-D.

It was a Disneyland-like production. It had the details of Pirates of the Caribbean. Most amazing about it all was that Pete made it happen so quickly.

Tina made a complete circle, stopping to pause at every booth as she listened to the sound effects from each attraction.

She marveled at the details. The reflection of the star in one of the wisemen's eyes; the straw inside the manger; the sawdust under a board where mechanical elves were working.

When she completed the circle, she returned to the entrance of the display and focused on the banner sign.

"Danny's Corner."

She read it again. "Danny's Corner."

It was hard to believe.

Pete could see she was starting to tear up.

"I remember holding Danny just before he died," Pete said. "I was trying to comfort him, keep him warm, talk to him."

Pete hadn't said anything to Tina about Danny's last few minutes of life. He wanted to save it for just the right moment.

"He wasn't in any pain. He wasn't crying. He was very calm. He wanted me to give this to his friend Cameron," Pete said pulling out a small present from his coat pocket.

"It was a present his father gave him. He said Santa didn't visit Cameron's house last year."

Tina nodded as though she knew the situation.

"He just wanted him to have a present," Pete said.

Tina marveled at her son's final act of selflessness. She wasn't surprised. He had always been too good to be true since he was just a little tyke. She knew he was something special.

"Tell me more," Tina pleaded.

"We talked about Christmas. The one thing he was worried about was missing Christmas. He talked about an idea for a present he was going to get you. He wondered if he was going to be home for Christmas. I told him he would be home. I promised him that."

"I would have given anything to be there for him," Tina said.

After a long pause Tina added, "How I wish I could have been there when he needed me."

There was a long pause as both Pete and Tina reflected on the situation. "I'm just so grateful you were there for him. I know you were chosen to look after him."

Pete never thought of it that way. Was it just a coincidence that his life had been touched by Danny? Or was it God's hand working through someone?

"The last thing I heard Danny say was almost like a whisper. I had to lean over next to his lips to hear him. He asked me one question. 'Why can't it last all year?'

"I spent a few days in the hospital after the crash. It never failed. Every night I'd repeat those words in my mind, over and over again as if I were trying to memorize them. 'Why can't Christmas last all year? Why?' Giving shouldn't be confined to a few weeks in December. Making children happy shouldn't be an annual event. It should happen every day. So I decided to try."

Pete grabbed Tina's hand and walked her toward the the tarp that covered the middle of Danny's Corner. He waved at one of the assistant managers, who pulled on the rope and lifted it up in the air toward the roof.

The first thing Tina saw was three steps that led to the wishing well centered in the middle of a round deck, big enough to hold a dozen people.

Then she noticed a bronze statue. It was of a boy. He had a smile on his face; the back of his hair poked up a little bit. It was Danny. A remarkable resemblance.

He was holding out a present. There was an inscription

next to Danny that read: Danny McMurtrey was a passenger on the ill-fated Flight 1392. He was one of many of our neighbors and friends who are no longer with us. There were 135 other people who died on Flight 1392. Danny's one wish was to Make Christmas last all year. Will you help?

On the side of the statue was a bronze sign with the list of names of each person who died on Flight 1392. It was a stunning tribute.

Tina reached out and touched the statue that was about four feet tall. She put her hands softly on its head and touched its face as if it were real.

She was overwhelmed. She walked up three steps and peered into the wishing well. There was a mirror under some shallow water that gave a reflection back to her.

"Excuse me, Pete. You've got a call. It's David Fletcher with the Tribune."

Pete figured Tina would want some time to herself, so he took the call and disappeared on the other side of Danny's Corner.

Tina reached into her purse and pulled out a fifty-cent piece. She looked back at the statue and closed her eyes.

A few minutes later she opened her eyes and tossed in the coin.

Chapter 19

The press conference was a hit. Even more media showed up than he anticipated. Even though the accident happened nearly three weeks ago, interest was still high. There were still many stories to be told.

The Chicago Tribune ran the story on the front page. David Fletcher told him that it would be a front page story on the phone when he reminded him of Pete's promise of a one-on-one interview—the first one-on-one interview.

The Sun Times teased the story off the front and led with it on its feature section.

NBC's Dateline called. The news show planned on doing a story to run on Christmas Eve.

The response Pete got from Danny's Corner surpassed all expectations. There was a line just to get in the store. Everyone wanted to see Danny's Corner.

Employees from another store were called in to help manage the crowds—to funnel the line to get in the store and the line to get into Danny's Corner.

So many employees signed up to volunteer to help there was even a waiting list.

Even the man with the "Golden Touch" was overwhelmed with its success.

It was now Wednesday, December 22. Danny's corner had been open for two days.

Pete was forced to limit the number of people that were allowed in to Danny's Corner to assure a positive experience for each child.

Donations from the first day reached a whopping $27,000 dollars.

In fact, in the two days that the Danny's Corner display had opened, the store had raised $47,000 in donations, including one anonymous $10,000 donation.

Pete made it clear that Sampson's would not take one penny for administration fees or anything else. One hundred percent of each donation would go to providing a better Christmas for those less fortunate.

The store had also been given over 500 names of families who needed help from as far away as California. Several were in neighboring states like Wisconsin, Iowa and Missouri. It was stunning. They just didn't have the manpower to pull this off.

At the very least, those who they couldn't get presents to in the next four days would each get a gift certificate in the mail and an invitation to come to Danny's Corner.

Finally, the rush of the last two weeks was beginning to ease up. Pete could see he was actually going to pull this off, much to the surprise of the management team at the store, who respectfully questioned his sanity.

It was Thursday, December 23, and now Tina faced the haunting realization of spending Christmas alone. She walked to her bare Christmas tree and picked up one of five presents under the tree and began unwrapping it.

She carefully peeled off the paper and held up the snow globe. How he would have loved this she thought.

Tina turned it upside down and shook it up, then watched the snowflakes slowly fall around Santa and on the ice rink.

The pain resurfaced. Emotionally, it had been a roller-coaster for the last three weeks which was capped off with the funeral, but Danny's Corner seemed to lift her spirits.

Now the finality of her loss, however, returned. The depression of her apartment was suffocating her.

She threw on her coat, gloves and scarf and walked out the door. She had to get out of her apartment. It was just getting dark. Winter had embraced Chicago like it always does. Her deep breaths were visible in the cold air. A slight chilling wind turned her nose red in just minutes. Snow flakes piled up on the top of her brown hair.

As Tina walked the streets, anger continued to build. Why Danny? There were over a hundred survivors, why wasn't he one of them? She thought about God. Why would he do this to her? He was all she had. Others had husbands, wives, other children, she had only Danny.

What had she done wrong? She believed she was a good person. She worked, went to school, helped Danny with his school work, never took him for granted. Even though she was often late on her payments, she'd always paid her debts and fulfilled her obligations, despite having hardly any help from Rick.

Was this her reward for trying to live a good life? Thinking about it, she felt it was as though Danny's death was meant to be.

She remembered hearing that the odds of dying in a plane crash are more than a million to one. Then, considering the other unlikely scenarios—like suddenly Rick coming up with enough money to fly him out. Then having Danny sit in the First Class section. Then, of all things, for Pete to switch seats with him.

It made no sense. It was like his time was up. How could that be? Tina wondered. How can the time of a seven-year old be up? Questions continued to stir. She'd been walking for an hour. It hadn't seemed like it. It wasn't very smart for her to be walking alone at night, but right now she didn't care. What could happen to her that could be worse than what she was already going through?

She had no fear. In fact, the thought of getting mugged and killed and put out of her misery was actually rather appealing. The pain would be over and she could be with Danny again.

She walked across a street with a blinking red hand, but she paid no attention to it. A car laid on its horn and despite the weather, the driver rolled down the window to curse her.

Tina wasn't fazed.

A corner building then caught her eye. There was a small neon sign that said, "Suicide Prevention Center."

She stared at the building, then decided to go in. Maybe there was someone there who could give her some tips, she said to herself in a sarcastic tone.

She tentatively opened the door and saw a woman talking on the phone. She looked up and raised her hand, acknowledging Tina's presence. She scribbled something on a note and handed it to Tina.

"Please make yourself comfortable. I'll be with you in a minute."

Tina looked around the small office. There were posters of support. "Your future is your friend."

"Live for today, live for tomorrow."

On the other side of the counter was a piece of paper that caught her attention. It had a number of suicide statistics.

Suicide is the ninth leading cause of death in the United States. In 1996, there were 31,130 people in the United States who died of HIV and there were 30,903 who committed suicide.

Wow, she had no idea.

She read on. There are usually warning signs. Seventy-five percent of those who commit suicide give warning signs to family and friends.

Women attempt suicide twice as often as men, but men actually end their own lives much more often than women—they're more successful—by a four-to-one clip.

Makes sense Tina thought. She didn't want to die. But she didn't want to live either. One thing she realized by wandering through the doors of the center—she knew she couldn't go through with it.

She looked up and saw a poem that was framed on the

wall.

> "God hath not promised skies always blue, flower-strewn pathways all our lives through. God hath not promised sun without rain, joy without sorrow, peace without pain.
>
> But God hath promised strength for the day, rest for the labor, light for the way. Grace for the trails, help from above, unfailing sympathy, undying love."

Tina reread the poem as she waited, absorbing each line.

"Sorry," the woman said. "It's been a busy night. There were supposed to be two other volunteers here tonight, but they didn't show up."

"Are you okay?" the woman continued.

Tina nodded, trying to keep her emotions in check.

The woman came up from behind the counter and said, "Please, have a seat."

She put her hand on Tina's. She had silver hair and wide, plastic-rimmed glasses.

"What can I do for you?"

Tina looked shocked. She paused and said, "I don't know. I'm not sure why I came in here. I was just out for a walk."

The woman said, "Do you have family members at home?"

Tina shook her head.

"Bingo," the woman thought. "Another case of holiday blues, another person alone for the holidays. Have you been feeling suicidal?"

"No, I don't think so, " Tina said. "I mean I've thought about it, but I haven't really gotten to that point."

The woman smiled.

"Do you want to tell me why you've been thinking about it?"

Tina paused again and didn't say a word. The woman could tell Tina was trying to compose herself to say the words.

"I lost my boy, and I don't know why."

The woman put her arm around Tina and patiently listened while Tina related how the last three weeks had transpired.

"Did you know the airlines have set up counseling sessions dear?"

"I know, but I don't see the point. They can't bring my boy back. That's the bottom line. They can say whatever they want, but nothing can change the fact that he's gone and he's never coming back."

"They have organized meetings for survivors and the passengers who have lost loved ones. I think it would be something that would help you."

Tina nodded and stood up when she heard the phone ring. She would go out and finish her walk.

"Wait," the woman said when she answered the phone.

Suddenly another phone rang.

Finally the light quit blinking and the person on the other line gave up.

"Would you like to set up a time when you could come in and see one of our counselors?" the woman asked. "There is no charge. Okay, please do that."

The woman hung up. "Sorry, it gets pretty busy at this time of the year."

The phone rang again. Then the other line lit up.

The woman picked up the first line. Then she whispered to Tina, "Would you just answer that and tell them I'll be right with them."

Tina picked up the phone with trepidation.

"Hello, Suicide Prevention."

Tina tried to say, "Can you hold?" but an older man on the other line was too hysterical to hear her. He began crying.

"It's happening again. I thought I could handle it, but I just can't. There's nothing for me to live for."

Tina talked to the man until the woman got off the other phone, then said, "I'm going to put you on the phone with..."

she paused and looked at her name tag, "Doris."

She passed off the phone and listened to her talk to the man. She could tell within a few minutes he had calmed down. Five minutes later she was off the phone.

"Thank you. You were really good. The man said how nice you were."

Tina smiled, picked up her gloves and started to button her coat.

"When you were a child, did you ever stand under a street light and try to catch the biggest snowflake you could see on your tongue?" Doris asked.

Tina nodded with a smile. "Yeah. I used to do that with Danny."

"What you probably never noticed was how many other snowflakes landed on your tongue while you tried to get the big one. That's what it's like working here. When you help one person, you're actually helping countless others that you never see and never hear from. But they are there. Trust me. They are there. A funny thing happens too. When you forget about your own problems to help someone else, your problems don't seem as burdensome."

Doris continued. "You know, we could use some help. Can you stay for another hour? We can talk and you could help me with the phones," she said as she handed Tina a card of "do's and don'ts" when talking to someone who is suicidal.

"I've got to get going," Tina said, giving herself an out.

The phone rang. "Okay, call me if you need to talk," Doris said.

Tina buttoned up her coat and slid on her gloves. Another phone rang. Guilt crept in. The woman had been so willing to help her. Surely, she could answer the phones for a few more minutes.

She took off her gloves and scanned the card.

Don't argue with them.
Don't say your suicide will hurt your family.
Don't say you have so much to live for.

Geeze, Tina wondered what she should say.
She then read the "Do's."

Tell them that you care.
Tell them they are not alone.
Tell them the suicidal feelings are only temporary.

That's all the time Tina had. She had to answer the phone before someone gave up. She picked up the phone and looked over at Doris, who gave her an encouraging smile.

"Hello, Suicide Prevention," Tina said. "Hello. Hello. Are you there?

Tina almost hung up but then she heard a soft, faint cry on the other line.

"Can, I help you?"

After another pause. "Hello, hello."

Tina took the phone away from her ear and nearly hung up, but just before she did a thought came firmly into her mind. "Be patient."

"Hello, I'm here to help," Tina said gently as she waited for a response.

Finally, a voice spoke on the other end of the line.

"No one can help. No one could possibly understand, not even my own husband."

"I'll try, if you give me a chance," Tina said.

"My life is over.... My daughter's dead. How can you change that? How can I live the rest of my life without her? What's the point?"

Tina instantly teared up and shocked the women with her response.

"I know. I feel the same way. My only son died 16 days and two hours ago. Sometimes I feel the same way. Most of the time I feel the same way."

Tina continued. "You remember that plane that crashed? My boy was on that flight. He'd gone to visit his father and was on his way home."

"Are you serious?" the woman asked.

"Yeah, these last two weeks have been the hardest time of my life. In fact, tonight I just went for a walk. I was thinking the same thing you were—that my life without Danny was over. That there was no point to going on.

"I don't work here. I just happened to be walking by and felt like I needed someone to talk to. So I came in and began talking with Doris, who is in charge here. It got kind of busy so she asked me to help her with the phones."

"My daughter was on that flight," the woman said.

Doris was now off the phone and listening to their conversation. She was pleasantly surprised to see how well Tina was handling herself.

She could tell whoever Tina was talking to, she was connecting with.

The conversation continued for another 20 minutes when the woman said something that stunned Tina.

"My Susie was the sunshine in our home. She was always so positive. No matter what kind of day she had, her favorite saying was, 'It's going to be a great day.' She'd always say that on her way out the door. That's how she approached each day. She was a sophomore at UCLA—she was coming home for Christmas."

"I don't believe it," Tina said in an astonished tone.

"What?"

"Do you know Pete Sampson?"

"Who?"

"Pete Sampson."

"No."

"He was on that flight. He sat next to my son. He told me what happened in the final few minutes before the plane crashed."

The woman didn't say a word, but her complete silence told Tina she was tuned in to every word.

"He told me about Susie..."

The woman interrupted. "How did he know her?"

"I don't think he did but he said this college girl with blonde hair that was wearing a UCLA sweatshirt gave my boy some gum and started a bubble-blowing contest."

"That's her," the woman said, laughing while crying, proving it is possible to do both at the same time.

"That's so her. I can just see her doing something like that."

Tina continued. "Pete said she could tell Danny was scared so she tried to take his mind off the situation. They laughed for a good five minutes and lightened up the mood on the entire plane."

"There's more," Tina continued. "Apparently the woman sitting next to Susie was emotionally having a hard time. She was crying loudly and at times almost hysterically. Pete said how impressed he was with Susie, because she held the woman's hand. She put her arm around her and tried to assure her that everything would be okay. He said your daughter was like an angel on board that flight. I can't tell you how much that means to me right now, that your daughter was so thoughtful."

"You're an answer to my prayers. I thank you," the woman said. "I'd like to talk to this Pete. Do you know how I can get a hold of him?"

"You know the airline has organized group meetings to help those involved in the tragedy?"

"I know, but I haven't had the strength to go."

"Me too," Tina said. "I never did get your name."

"It's Robyn."

"Listen, Robyn, I've got a perfect idea. Meet me at Sampson's Department Store on Michigan Ave. tomorrow at 5:00 p.m. Can you?"

The woman hesitated, so Tina explained more. "I have something you must see. Pete is the CEO of Sampson's Department Stores. He's done something very special for those on Flight 1392. I'd like you to see it."

"I'll be there. I promise."

Chapter 20

Christmas Eve at Sampson's was a complete zoo. The publicity Danny's Corner brought coupled with a strong economy had the aisles at Sampson's packed like an interstate at rush hour.

Pete was sure December would smash sales for the store, but he was more concerned with the success of Danny's Corner. He envisioned a place where shoppers could come and spend a few minutes, a place where he could bring a little holiday cheer to those who had little to cheer about. And at the same time it would be something he could do to keep his promise to Danny—to help make Christmas not only better for Cam but to help it last all year.

But not even Pete was prepared for the tremendous success of Danny's Corner.

There was always a line outside the section of the store. He felt like The Grinch That Stole Christmas when he was forced to limit the time each kid had in Danny's Corner to 30 minutes, but the sheer numbers left him with no choice.

Pete had a big night planned. He narrowed the list down to 200 names that were within a 40-mile radius around the store, so it would physically be possible to make so many rounds. After all, he wasn't Santa. The rest would get Sampson gift certificates. He felt guilty, but next year he promised himself he would have time to do more.

The plan was to use five different Sampson trucks to split up the routes. But a Christmas Eve delivery proved to be a difficult sell. Employees, who had been great about volunteering in Danny's Corner, had families to spend Christmas Eve with. As a result he was 15 volunteers short.

That's okay, Pete thought. He'd do it all himself if he had to. Even if he finished on Christmas afternoon. All the families would be seen. That much he promised himself.

There were a few extra cars outside when Robyn pulled in her driveway from her first trip outside the house since the funeral.

She recognized the cars.

She opened the garage door that led to the kitchen and found her family sitting around the table. Kyle and Megan were sitting next to her husband Paul along with his sister and her husband (their kids were playing in the other room), her youngest brother and her closest friend and her husband. The Moores, who lived across the street, had also come over.

It was obvious they had been talking about her, because when she came in the room the talk went silent.

The group offered a loving smile at her.

"What's going on?" Robyn asked.

"I made some cookies and holiday junk..." Just then Megan cut in by clearing her throat. "Uh, hem."

"Oh, I had some help," Paul said.

"Some help? I made the cookies and the fudge. You and Kyle were just the taste testers."

"Hey, I helped," Kyle protested.

"Yeah, lick the bowl."

"Let's just say it was a team effort," Paul said, cutting in.

"How thoughtful," Robyn said. "Thank you."

"Wow," Kyle thought. He wasn't sure having so many people over was such a good idea, but clearly Mom was in the best mood he'd seen her in since the accident.

The group began to break up into the living room. It was now 4:00 p.m.

"So do you have any plans tonight?" Robyn's friend Denise said.

"Now I do."

Robyn began to talk about the excitement at Sampson's Department Store.

Now the others had all migrated into the living room and somehow all the attention was on Robyn and Denise's conversation.

"I met this woman who lost her boy on the flight," Denise said. "She was telling me about this man who is the CEO of Sampson's. He was on Flight 1392 and apparently he's done some sort of dedication to those on the plane. He mentioned Susie."

Denise looked surprised.

"This woman asked me to come down to Sampson's tonight so she could show me something," Robyn said.

After a slight pause, Robyn came up with an idea. "Hey, why don't we all go down? I'm meeting her there at 5:00 p.m. We could all go."

There was some hesitation by the group, but Paul quickly lent support to her idea.

"Yeah, we could do some last minute Christmas shopping."

"Sounds good," Robyn's sister added.

"What time should we be there?" her brother asked.

"Five."

Chapter 21

The sign on the door of Sampson's Department Store read, "We will be closing at 7:30 p.m. on Christmas Eve so our employees can spend time with their families."

It was now 5:00 p.m. and judging by the crowd of people packed in the store, procrastination was alive and well in Chicago. Every register was open and there was a line forming on each register, even the ones set up for "Cash Only."

It was obvious by the number of shoppers that Sampson's would be turning away customers when it was time to close.

For the most part, Danny's Corner was already closed. The booths were unmanned. The gate, however, was unlocked. The only section not closed off was the path that led to the wishing well and the memorial.

Pete was busy picking up colored sheets of paper off the floor. There was frosting smeared on several chairs and tables—wiping down the tables was next on his list. He'd hoped to solicit some help from the store employees, but that never happened. All available employees were needed to handle the rush of last-minute Christmas shoppers.

He did have four volunteers, who requested the night off, but then agreed to come down to the store anyway and help load the trucks with toys.

While he was disappointed with the disappearance of some volunteers, Pete found the spirit of the Christmas season continued to thrive in Danny's Corner.

"Gina! What are you doing here?" Pete asked.

"I saw you on TV. I had to come down and see if you needed some help."

Pete gave her a meaningful embrace like she was a family member. In a sense she was. Everyone on Flight 1392 was now like family.

Gina joined Pete in cleaning off the tables. They worked on the final table together when Gina looked up and asked Pete something that was bothering her.

"So why are you doing all this?" Gina asked.

After her experience on the plane, she wondered if this was another one of Pete's business schemes—a new wrinkle to increase sales.

The question shocked Pete. Gina's skepticism could be heard in her voice.

Pete paused while he assessed his feelings.

"When you hold a seven-year-old boy in your arms and watch him die, the world suddenly looks completely different.

"It's like someone changed the rules to Monopoly. Instead of trying to hoard all the money and bankrupt your neighbor, the game is how many people you can help along the way.

"You want to know what Danny asked me just before he died?" Pete said in a defensive tone.

Gina just looked at Pete and nodded.

"He wanted to know why Christmas can't last all year? But I'm convinced what Danny loved about Christmas wasn't the presents he had to open on Christmas morning. It was the spirit of the season he loved. That's what's addicting—the spirit of the season.

"He loved making decorations for his Christmas tree with his mom. He loved frosting sugar cookies and giving them to his neighbors. He loved being loved."

Gina could see Pete was sincere. She felt bad now that she had almost accused Pete of creating Danny's Corner for ulterior motives.

Pete's cheeks were red. His commitment was visible on his face. He paused as he struggled to keep his composure.

"I made him a promise. I promised Danny it would last all year."

Gina grabbed Pete's hand in a gesture of comfort. She could tell how much Danny's Corner meant to Pete.

Pete looked up and saw Tina, leading a large group of people toward them like he'd just opened up a new register and said, "I can help whoever's next down here."

Pete walked over to the counter where the sink was, washed his hands and tossed a paper towel in the garbage and prepared to greet Tina.

She went right to Pete and gave him a hug and a kiss on the cheek.

Then he introduced her to Gina.

Tina knew by the description Pete had given her that Gina was the flight attendant that looked after Danny. She smiled and felt strengthened by Gina's presence. She couldn't wait to find the right moment to talk to her.

"These are some special friends," Tina said pointing to the group led by Robyn.

Instead of being bothered by the surprise, Pete was in top social form, the type it takes to be a successful CEO. He shook every hand and smiled as he was introduced.

When he got to Robyn, he sensed she had come to see the memorial. Robyn teared up and held onto his handshake so long it began to be uncomfortable.

"Welcome," Pete said. "This is what we call 'Danny's Corner.'"

Pete introduced so many people to Danny's Corner and had told the story so many times he made no mistakes and sounded like a polished tour guide.

"As you know. We lost many neighbors and dear friends with the crash of Flight 1392. We lost husbands, wives, brothers, sisters, sons and daughters, neighbors and friends. Nothing can ever take their place, but what we can do is remember. We can remember what they brought to our lives. We can remember their love and how they made each day of our lives that much richer. We will remember because we can never forget."

Tina cut in. "The name of each person that died on Flight 1392 is engraved in the bronze plate centered in the middle of a large rock by the wishing well."

Robyn led the group to the brass plate. She used her index finger to go down the list of names.

Finally, about half-way down, her finger stopped. "Susan Sperry."

Paul knelt beside her and slipped his arm around her.

Tina had backed away from the group and was now telling Pete and Gina who Robyn was.

"Remember the college girl from UCLA—the blonde that was in a bubble blowing contest with Danny..."

Tina nodded toward Robyn's direction. Now he could see the resemblance. From the blonde hair to the small pointy nose, to the big blue eyes.

Pete sighed in sympathy.

Robyn stopped at the wishing well, tossed in a coin and paused to marvel at the statue of Danny as she seemed fascinated with the inscription.

Pete reverently approached her. "Are all these people family members?"

Robyn nodded. "And close friends."

The group began making its way back to Tina and Pete.

"We have some special Christmas Eve goodies set up over there," Pete said as he pointed to an adjacent room.

"I'd like to invite everyone to move over and get some eggnog and cookies before you go."

Tina led the group toward the room. Robyn waited behind. Pete knew what she wanted.

She looked at the booths that were deserted, hoping Pete would notice.

"You know your daughter was a bright light in the darkest of situations. I know this is a hard time for you. But you should be proud. Of the 300 plus passengers on that flight, no one was more caring and sensitive to the needs of others in those last final minutes than she was," Pete paused slightly, then added, "No one."

Robyn nodded in appreciation.

"She was like an angel on board."

After another speechless pause, Pete said, "Come on, let's go back to the wishing well and I'll tell you about it."

A grateful mother walked to the wishing well, already having one wish come true.

The rest of the group made a small but noticeable dent in the eggnog bowl. Sandwiches had just arrived. Pete wanted to make sure those who volunteered on Christmas Eve would have a positive experience and no one is happy if they're hungry.

Thirty minutes later Pete and Robyn joined the rest of the group.

"Ah, the sandwiches arrived. Good," Pete said. "You all can have some. I'm sure there will be plenty left over."

"What's this all for?" Robyn's brother Luke asked?

"Thanks to donations from Danny's Corner, we're delivering five trucks full of presents to families in our area that otherwise would have had little or no Christmas at all. I've ordered some refreshments for those who have volunteered to help."

"When are you getting started?" Paul asked.

"Two trucks have already left. We're a little shorthanded on the other three, so we might have to wait until the crew from one of the other trucks gets back before we roll these other three out on the street."

Pete picked up a clipboard on the wall and lifted up a page. "You never know what kind of turnout you're going to get on Christmas Eve. A lot of people signed up but didn't show up."

"Mr. Sampson. I'd like to stay and help. Do you have anything I can do?" Robyn asked.

Kyle looked at Megan like his mother was crazy.

"You bet, if you're sure you're up to it."

One by one members of the group began to speak up. "We can stay too."

The spirit of the season mixed with the peer pressure of the situation was like a chain reaction of dominoes.

Tina cut in. "I can't drive one of these trucks, but I'm a pretty good navigator."

Everyone had offered to help except Luke, who nudged his wife and subtly shook his head. They'd been married for five years and had no kids. But long enough to know he was against the idea. Dinner was waiting at home. They'd rented movies and planned on spending a quiet romantic evening at home.

But the wife ignored Luke's hint and when it came her turn to stay or go, said, "We'd love to stay and help."

Pete split up the volunteers into three groups. The only question was where to put Gina. He wanted her to come with him, but knew Gina's presence was exactly what Robyn and her family needed.

Pete had been short 15 volunteers. Now he had 16.

Chapter 22

Luke and his wife Shannon followed the delivery truck in their car.

"What were you thinking? We had plans tonight," he said scolding Shannon for getting them into this mess.

"We can still do what we have planned. So what if we start it later?"

"Yeah, but by 11 o'clock I'll be too tired."

"Then we can do it Christmas night."

Luke didn't respond, he just gave her a disapproving look and sighed when someone slipped into the parking place he was going for.

"Figures," he mumbled.

Pete opened the door and helped Tina and their helper into the delivery truck.

"So what's your name?" Tina asked.

"Trevor," the boy replied.

"Is it okay if Trevor rides up in the front with us?" Pete asked the Moores, Robyn's neighbors.

"That's great, we'll follow you," Mr. Moore said.

Pete, Trevor and Tina waved to the Moores as the truck pulled away. The truck Pete used for delivery belonged to one of the stores. It was about the size of a UPS truck, but instead of colored UPS brown and yellow, the Sampson's truck was like the yellow of a Rider truck.

There was a reason Pete wanted to drive this truck. The

lettering said "Sampson's" on both sides, but it also had a new look. Pete had just added "Danny's Corner" on the back. He knew Tina would like it.

There was a break in the snow. It was now just Chicago-style cold, with a slight breeze coming off Lake Michigan. The temperature was down to 12 degrees.

"So how old are you, Trevor? You look like you're about ten or eleven."

He smiled and said, "How'd you know?"

"Well," Pete said. Which one is it. Fourteen or fifteen?"

Trevor giggled. "Nah, I'm only ten and a half."

"So are you going to have a great Christmas?" Tina asked.

"Yeah, it's going to be great. I have this huge present under the tree, well sort of under it. It's too big to go under it. But I can't wait to open it. I'm going to open it first. I'll bet it's a bike."

"You know what we're doing tonight?" Tina asked.

Trevor had an idea, but instead he shrugged his shoulders. He was more focused on riding in the truck than where they were going and what they were going to do.

"We're going to deliver presents to lots of kids who don't have a big present like yours under the tree. In fact, many of the people we're going to visit don't have any presents at all," Tina added.

"That sounds fun," Trevor said. "Can I deliver some."

"Sure," Pete said, putting his arm on his neck.

Luke and Shannon's first stop was St. Mark's Hospital, floor two—the children's floor.

There were a few homemade decorations on the wall and a little tree on the counter of the nurse's station, but other than that, the hospital showed no signs of Christmas Eve.

Luke was surprised. He didn't know what to expect, but somehow he thought it would be different.

There were five of them altogether that separated from

the others. Two of the three volunteers from Sampson's stayed in the truck mapping out their next stop, while the other three, Luke, Shannon and the designated volunteer—dressed up in a Santa suit—checked in at the nurse's station.

He pulled out a list of room numbers. There were three nurses at the desk. All seemed pleased at their presence.

"Room 222, we'll go there first," Santa said.

"Do, do, do, do," Luke started whistling the theme song from the old TV series.

Shannon looked at him in a disapproving way. "It's room 222 you know. I've been watching the reruns on TV Land."

"Okay, never mind," Luke said shaking his head. "Geeze, no one appreciates a little laugh."

He looked down at his watch. 7:15 p.m. This is going to take all night he mumbled to himself. Why are we even here? There's two guys out in the truck that could help carry Santa's bags. It's one thing if they really needed me, he thought as he lagged behind Santa and Shannon as if he weren't part of the group. Santa pulled out a piece of paper, then stashed it back in his pocket.

"Ho, ho, ho, Merry Christmas, Mary. Merry Christmas."

An eight year-old girl was surrounded by her mother and father. She looked up when Santa came into the room.

It was obvious the girl had been crying. But not now. Instantly the sight of Santa stopped her tears.

"I thought I might find you here," Santa said. "Ho, ho. I think this is a great place to spend Christmas. Where else do you get room service and breakfast in bed?"

The girl laughed and her parents smiled.

"Yeah, but the food is yucky."

"I thought it might be, so I brought you an early present." Santa pulled out a box of chocolates.

"Sssh. Don't tell the nurses. They'll get mad at me. And don't let mom and dad eat them all."

Mary giggled again and put the box of chocolates by her side.

"How you feelin'?" Santa asked.

"I'm okay. I just want to go home."

Not sure what to say, Santa just gave her a sympathetic smile.

"I've brought some helpers with me," Santa said as he looked back at Luke and Shannon, each holding a red bag of gifts.

"They don't look like elves," Mary said.

"Look a little closer, Luke has pointed ears, see?" Santa said, pointing at Luke's ears that were partially hidden by the Chicago Bears hat he was wearing.

Luke laughed and shewed Santa away.

Shannon reached into her bag and handed the girl a present wrapped in shiny red paper and decorated with a gold-colored ribbon and bow.

"Ah, ah, ahh. You have to wait until Christmas," Santa said.

"Oh, come on Santa."

"I'll tell you what," Santa said reaching into his bag. "You can open this one tonight."

Santa leaned over and gave Mary a hug. "Merry Christmas sweetie. I hope you get better real soon."

Shannon put her arm on Mary's shoulder and said, "Merry Christmas."

Luke was a little uncomfortable with the situation and just waved as they walked out the door.

The rounds continued. Room after room they went until they came to the final room on the floor.

It was the saddest of all the sights.

A nurse followed the three in the room.

The room was empty except for the small withered body of a twelve-year-old boy.

His hair was shaved. An IV ran out of his left hand. A pair of tubes ran into a mask that covered his nose. His whole face was pale and swollen.

The nurse whispered. "He's recovering from surgery. A brain tumor."

Santa whispered, "Is it okay? Should I..."

She nodded and said, "I think a few minutes would be fine."

Santa shook his bells reluctantly, still a little unsure that he was doing the right thing.

"Ho, ho, young Corey. Merry Christmas."

The boy blinked his eyes, squinted, then focused on Santa.

Santa put his finger up toward his lips. "Shhh. You don't have to say a word. Don't try and talk."

The boy nodded.

"You didn't think I'd forget about you? I brought you a special present."

Santa pulled out a wrapped puzzle. That would be perfect for his recovery.

He'd been saving one of the biggest presents for the person that he felt needed it the most.

Surely no one deserved it more. No one needed it more. He pulled out a Nintendo Game Boy wrapped in solid dark red paper, decorated with a white bow on it.

"I think you're really going to like this one," he said shaking the present.

"Ah, and this is Luke, he has another present for you. We had so many presents for you, old Santa couldn't carry them all. I'll have to eat some more cookies. I'm getting to be a lightweight."

Luke leaned forward and showed the boy a present. He didn't move his head but his innocent eyes followed his every action.

Luke mouthed, "For you."

He set it on the table next to his bed. Then he turned his head to hide his tears.

He quickly wiped them off his face and cleared his throat as if to hide his secret. It was no use. Shannon could see he was struggling.

Santa slung the empty sack over his shoulder and nodded for Shannon and Luke to go.

Santa's white gloves held one of the boy's hands. Shannon held the other.

"I'll be checking up on you. So get better and that's an order."

The trio headed for the door while the nurse stayed behind to check Corey's vital signs.

"Merry Christmas," the three said in harmony.

"Merry Christmas," Luke said in a soft and gentle tone.

They walked down the halls of the second floor to the elevator with Santa leading the way.

Luke came up from behind Shannon, slipped his arm around her and whispered in her ear.

"Thanks."

Shannon nodded and smiled.

Chapter 23

"Trevor, are you having fun?" Tina asked.

"Yeah, it's great helping Santa."

They had one more stop.

It was 10:10 p.m. Christmas Eve. The streets were now nearly deserted. A light snow was falling. The people of Chicago had settled in for Christmas.

Pete, or Santa, pulled the truck up to a small white rundown house. It was a different colored white than the snow that was on the ground. The house was a darker white, a dirtier white. The color of white that you'd see if you forgot to add laundry soap to a batch of white laundry.

The snow on the roof hid the weather-worn shingles well. It was too cold for the water to drip in the kitchen where it usually dripped from the window seal and into the kitchen sink.

"Go ahead and ring the doorbell," Pete told Trevor.

Trevor took off the glove on his right hand and pushed the doorbell, but all that was left in the doorbell was a tiny light and a round circle. It obviously didn't work.

Trevor knocked softly.

Pete followed, "Boom, boom, boom," three swift, sure knocks. Then he shook the bells on his belt.

The door opened slowly. Then the eyes of a little boy lit up.

"Santa."

"Ho, ho, ho. You waitin'' up for Santa are you?"

He eagerly nodded his head yes.

Three more kids ran toward the door. Pete figured the littlest one was about four or five, while the others looked like they couldn't have been older than ten.

"I brought you all some presents. Is your mom home?"

A teenage girl emerged from the kitchen and viewed Santa and Trevor with skepticism, until she saw the familiar face of Tina.

There was a Christmas tree in the corner of the room. It was the sorriest tree Pete had ever seen. It looked like it was a branch cut off one of the big trees downtown. It looked like about half of the green needles had turned brown and fallen to the floor.

Under the tree were five or six presents. But none of them were bigger than a shoe box. It looked like a pair of socks, maybe a shirt or some pants wrapped up.

Two more kids came from the kitchen, bringing the count to eight.

The teenage girl tempered the excitement of the little ones, by cutting in, "She's not here. She's working."

One of the kids pulled Pete's arm and another tugged on Santa's hand clutching his white gloves.

They pulled him over to an oversize chair that had duck tape on the seat, trying to keep the tear in the seat from getting any bigger.

One of the kids brought out some cookies they made just in case Santa came this year.

While the kids gathered around Santa to offer him a plate of cookies, Tina quietly disappeared out the door.

Pete had two bags of toys left with about 20 presents left over. It was clear this would be the best Christmas present this family would ever have.

He took turns talking to each child as they sat on his lap and gave them a present.

When he'd given out all the presents in his bag, he introduced Trevor, who was holding the other sack.

"This is Rudolph; he's my special helper."

"Hey, he doesn't have a red nose," one of the boys questioned.

"Yeah, and Rudolph is a reindeer, Santa," one of the girls said as she giggled.

"No, no, no. Not the reindeer, silly. Rudolph the elf, Santa's special helper. Who do you think Rudolph was named after?"

"Oohhh."

Trevor beamed. The attention made him feel important, not out of place.

Trevor handed out the rest of the presents under Santa's direction.

Tina slipped back in the door, her reappearance lost in the excitement of passing out the presents.

"Is that Donner?" one of the kids asked when Tina was spotted closing the door.

Tina didn't understand what all the laughing was about. By the way Trevor and Pete were laughing, she figured it was an inside joke. She just smiled and pretended she got the punch line.

"I know, it's Mrs. Claus," another child said.

"That's right," Tina said. "I've come along this year to monitor how many cookies Santa eats," she said patting him on the belly. "As you can see, last year he had a few too many."

"Ho, ho, ho," Pete said. "But they were so good."

There was a reason this house was the last stop on the night. Tina couldn't hear what Pete was saying, but he took Cameron on his lap and pulled out a small present wrapped in Forest Green paper. He could see Pete was whispering something into his ear.

He nodded and gave him a hug as he unwrapped the present.

When Cam's turn was up on Santa's lap, Tina waved Cameron over to her.

"I've got something for you. It means a lot to me. I think

it's the neatest thing in the whole world. I hope you think so too. Do you have a tradition where you can open up one present on Christmas Eve?"

Cam shook his head.

"Well now you do."

Tina uncovered the snow globe that was inside a sack.

Cam's eyes went into shock.

"Wow!" he looked at Tina as if he were asking permission to touch it.

She nodded and extended the snow globe to him.

He clutched it with both hands for a few seconds then held it up to his face, so close that his nose touched the glass.

"Look, " Tina said as she grabbed the snow globe and shook it as she turned it upside down.

Large snowflakes fell covering the ice rink where the miniature people were skating. Even though the snowflakes were falling, you could still see the smile on the boy's face as he sat on Santa's lap.

The detail was magnificent.

The other children gathered round to see what the excitement was all about.

Tina smiled as she saw the attention the whole family had given the present—the present she thought would be perfect for Danny.

How he would have loved it. She always planned on saving the snow globe as a reminder of Danny. But tonight, when she walked in this house, she changed her mind. Somehow she knew this is what Danny would have wanted. Besides, there were plenty of other souvenirs of Danny's life.

Cameron, who had only played over at Tina's house two or three times, gave up the snow globe to the others and came over to give Tina a hug.

"Thank you for coming."

Tina's heart stopped. That voice.

Tina pulled the boy back.

"What did you say? He just looked at her like he'd said something wrong.

"Did you just say something?" Tina asked again.

"Thank you."

There was nothing in the voice that stirred her heart this time.

Perhaps it was a faint message from a distant place. Just subtle enough to be understood.

"Hello, hello," a loud voice came from the doorway.

"Well my goodness, looky here."

"Mom," the kids yelled. "Look what I got."

"Mom, Santa came."

It was like the family was running a fire drill. Kids were running around the room screaming—with excitement, not fear—and the joy of the season sparked a fire in everyone's heart.

While Pete took the opportunity to fill Mom in on what they had been doing, Tina motioned to Pete that she would be outside.Tina quietly shut the door behind her. The snow was falling once again, much harder now than it had before. The streets were now in need of a snow plow.

Tina walked about a block down the street where there was a street light.

She looked up at the light and was quickly mesmerized by the falling snowflakes. She tried to focus on one, but when she did, several snowflakes landed in her eyes.

Tina blinked and wiped the snow off her eyes. She then looked up at the light one more time. There it was. She noticed an oversized snowflake, at least three times the size of any of the others.

She followed it from the top of the street light as it floated slowly down like a feather with a parachute. She felt as if she were in the snow globe.

Tina held out her tongue and closed her eyes. She could feel the snowflake make contact with her tongue.

What she didn't notice was that five other snowflakes had also landed on her tongue.

The voice returned. She could hear it as she tightened

her closed eyes. "Merry Christmas, Mom."

Tina opened her eyes and stared up at the street light again, then began to laugh.

"Merry Christmas, Danny."

—The End